"I don't expect anything from you." Cory gave a quiet laugh.

"Lowering my expectations has become par for the course these days. If you want to be a part of his life—"

"Who do you think I am?" Jordan demanded, temper flaring again. "Hell yes, I want to be a part of his life, Cory. He's my son. I don't know how we're going to figure this out, but I can guaran-damn-tee you that I'm not letting him go."

"Okay," she said. "We'll find a way to make it work. Gran always said everything is figureoutable. I believe that."

She spoke softly, her tone calm, like she was trying to gentle an angry bear. Jordan sighed when he realized he was the bear. Another benefit of his simple life was that it allowed him to stay in control of his emotions. When he didn't feel much of anything, he couldn't get himself into trouble.

Tonight a bomb had gone off, blowing apart the simple life he'd crafted in Starlight. Despite Cory's vow to make it work, he had no doubt that his moratorium on trouble had just been lifted.

Dear Reader,

One of the greatest joys of my life is being a mom. So when I created the character of Cory Hall—a determined single mom who is working to make something great of her life in order to provide for her son and be a role model to him—her love and dedication were something I related to on a personal level.

Cory has made mistakes and has been knocked down a bit by life, but she never gives up trying to do the right thing. Even when the right thing is tracking down her baby's father and revealing to Starlight bar owner Jordan Schaeffer that he has a son he didn't know about.

Since leaving the spotlight of professional football, Jordan has created a simple life for himself in the small town nestled in the Cascade Mountains of central Washington. He lives a solitary existence when not tending bar but has told himself that he's content that way. But he's never forgotten the woman who captured his heart during their brief friendship, and Cory's return shakes his world to its foundation.

Jordan didn't expect to become a father and Cory isn't looking for love, but when these two bruised souls come together for the sake of their son, they might discover a future better than they ever imagined.

I hope you enjoy this return to Starlight and I would love to hear from you. Find me on Facebook, Instagram or at www.michellemajor.com.

Hugs,

Michelle

His Secret
Starlight Baby

MICHELLE MAJOR

HARLEQUIN

SPECIAL
EDITION

HARLEQUIN®
SPECIAL EDITION™

Recycling programs
for this product may
not exist in your area.

ISBN-13: 978-1-335-40470-1

His Secret Starlight Baby

Copyright © 2021 by Michelle Major

This edition published by arrangement with Harlequin Books S.A.

For questions and comments about the quality of this book,
please contact us at CustomerService@Harlequin.com.

Harlequin Enterprises ULC
22 Adelaide St. West, 40th Floor
Toronto, Ontario M5H 4E3, Canada
www.Harlequin.com

Printed in U.S.A.

Michelle Major grew up in Ohio but dreamed of living in the mountains. Soon after graduating with a degree in journalism, she pointed her car west and settled in Colorado. Her life and house are filled with one great husband, two beautiful kids, a few furry pets and several well-behaved reptiles. She's grateful to have found her passion writing stories with happy endings. Michelle loves to hear from her readers at michellemajor.com.

To Dutch—
Thanks for being a fantastic father-in-law and
for raising one of the best men I know (and love!).

Chapter One

Cory Hall approached the man who'd just exited the darkened bar, trying not to be intimidated by his size and strength. He was well over six feet tall with an athlete's build, the body of a former NFL star.

In the dim glow of the streetlamp overhead, it was hard to make out his features, although she knew his dark hair was shot through with streaks of burnished gold, the kind of natural highlights that pro-athlete wives and girlfriends spent gobs of money to re-create in the salon. Cory could see that his angular jaw was muted by several days of stubble, and the canvas jacket he wore strained to envelop his massive shoulders.

He turned back toward the door without noticing

her. At this point in her life, she was used to being invisible, so that wasn't a surprise.

"We're closed," he said, his voice reverberating in the quiet of the hour. So he'd noticed her after all. He didn't bother to turn from the door he was locking. Either Jordan Schaeffer didn't expect trouble late at night in a small town like Starlight, Washington, or he wasn't worried about handling himself.

It could be either option. Yet Cory was about to dump a whole heap of trouble into his life that might make him wish he'd taken more care.

She certainly would have made different choices if someone offered her a do-over on the past few years. More care with her heart and a sharper focus on what she wanted her life to look like. Instead, Cory had let the people around her dictate her choices and her self-worth, and they hadn't given a single damn about her. Now she was ready to begin again at twenty-seven years old. There was only one thing that mattered—her baby—and she'd do whatever it took to be the mom he deserved.

After a quick glance over her shoulder at her grandmother's old Buick, which was parked at the curb, Cory swallowed and took another step forward.

"Hey, Jordan."

His hand stilled on the set of keys he held, and his broad back went stiff. For a moment Cory didn't think that he recognized her voice. A spike of panic zinged across her middle at the thought he might not even remember her.

They hadn't exactly parted as the best of friends.

A bitter wind whistled along the empty street, and she hugged her arms tight across her body. She'd left her big coat in the car when the anticipation of this meeting left her drenched in sweat. The late-March temperature was cool but not frigid, not like the biting cold of her hometown in Michigan. This part of Washington, an hour east of Seattle in a valley at the base of the Cascade Mountains, had appeared both temperate and picturesque when she'd driven in earlier this afternoon. In fact, it seemed perfect. A quaint, quiet place to start fresh.

Cory needed a fresh start like she needed her next breath.

Jordan went back to locking the door, and if it weren't for that initial rigidity and the tension currently radiating from him, Cory might have thought he hadn't heard her greeting.

When he turned, she realized what a fool she'd been—nothing new there. Jordan's pale green eyes blazed with an emotion she couldn't name, although it definitely wasn't friendly. Not that she expected a warm welcome back into his life, although she had to admit, in the two and a half days it had taken to drive halfway across the country, her mind had wandered down the path of silly fantasy more than once.

She fisted her hands, the sharp pain of nails stabbing into the flesh of her palm a much-needed reminder to stay grounded in reality. Cory was in Starlight to take care of business, not to indulge in ridiculous daydreams. Single moms didn't have time for that sort of nonsense.

"How are you?" she asked, clearing her throat when the words came out on a croak. She tried for a smile. "It's been a minute."

"What are you doing here?" He pocketed the set of keys and rocked back on his heels. His eyes raked over her in a way that left her wishing she hadn't forgotten her flat iron back in Michigan. Or had she deserted that particular styling tool when she'd taken off from Atlanta? She hadn't given much thought to making herself look pretty in what felt like ages.

"I was...um...in the area, and I thought I'd stop in and say hi." She gave a limp wave. "Hi."

Jordan stared at her like she'd lost her mind.

"I didn't know if you'd remember me." She pushed away a stray lock of hair that blew into her face. "I'm sure you want to—"

"I remember, Cory." His voice was a deep, angry rumble. "I remember everything."

She swallowed. "Oh. Okay, well, that's good. I think." She gestured to the bar he'd exited minutes earlier. "You own this place, right? It looks nice." She inwardly cringed at her inability to stem the tide of inane babble pouring from her mouth. She wasn't here for pleasantries but couldn't quite bring herself to get to the point.

"It's after midnight." He ran a hand through his thick hair. She still couldn't see its true color, but it was longer than he'd worn it when he'd played football in Georgia. Untamed and a bit wild, much like the man himself.

"Right." She took a slow, steadying breath. "I need to talk to you, Jordan."

"I got that."

"It's about what happened when you left."

"From what I saw on ESPN, Kade got one hell of a contract offer. Forty million for four years. He got it all. You both got exactly what you wanted."

She winced at the accusation in his voice, even though she deserved every bit of judgment and condemnation Jordan Schaeffer could dish out. "Kade and I aren't together," she said, as if that explained everything when it was only the tip of the iceberg.

"Not my concern, Cory. In fact, right now my only concern is getting home and into bed for a decent night's sleep. I wish you well in whatever you choose for life after Kade Barrington, if you're telling the truth about that."

"I never lied," she said, trying and mostly failing to keep the pain out of her voice. Trying and completely failing to stop an image of Jordan asleep in bed from filling her mind.

"You went back to him."

Cory sucked in a shaky gulp of air, because she could have sworn she heard an answering pain in Jordan's tone. That couldn't be possible, because...

"After you took off." She bit down on the inside of her cheek until she tasted blood. "You left without even saying goodbye."

He laughed, a harsh scrape across her fraught nerves. "Sweetheart, we barely said hello."

Oh no. He wasn't going to do that. Not now. Not after everything Cory had dealt with in the past year. She might have had only one night with Jordan, but it had meant...something. To her, it had turned out to mean everything.

Her gaze darted to the gas guzzler her grandmother had given her before she died last month, and Cory was tempted to walk away. She could climb back in the car, spend one night in the local inn where she'd rented a room and be on the highway by first light.

Then she looked at him again, at those unique eyes she saw staring back at her every day, and realized she had to see this through. If not for herself, then for her baby.

"We said plenty," she told him, straightening her shoulders. "We did plenty. Enough that I have a six-month-old son in that car." She hitched a finger at the Buick. "You have a son, Jordan."

Jordan stared at the little boy gazing up at him from his mother's arms for several long seconds, then resumed pacing back and forth across the scuffed hardwood of Trophy Room, the bar he owned.

His mind continued to race at a thousand miles an hour, and adrenaline pumped through him so hard he thought his head might actually explode. Jordan had grown up an athlete. He could handle adrenaline. On the football field, he'd loved the spike of heat through his veins. It meant he was ready for action. He was in control. It didn't matter whom he was facing in the lineup or what the stakes were, from his chance at a college scholarship to a national championship to a televised playoff game.

He rose to meet every challenge and welcomed each new opponent, unwavering in his faith that determination and dedication would see him through.

Cory Hall had nearly felled him with four simple words.

You have a son.

Of course he remembered her. The thought that he could forget the sweet, beautiful woman who'd been the girlfriend of Jordan's jerk-wad quarterback was preposterous. She was different from a lot of the other girlfriends and wives on the team. She didn't seem to care much about the trappings of the lifestyle, only about keeping Kade happy, which turned out to be no easy task.

Jordan had played with Kade Barrington in Atlanta for two seasons and had been more than a little shocked that a woman like Cory could be so devoted.

Kade had talent in spades, but he'd been released from the team that drafted him out of college due to his inability to get along with the coaches and other players.

He landed in Atlanta with an attitude and something to prove. He and Cory had rented a big house in an expensive neighborhood, and Kade had loved to throw huge team parties. Cory had never seemed all that comfortable in big groups, which was how she and Jordan had ended up talking late one night out by the pool.

Their talks had become a bright spot in his otherwise dark life. Then he'd been injured and hadn't seen her for months. Until the night she showed up at his condo after breaking up with Kade. She'd asked to sleep on his sofa, and he still believed that was what they'd both intended.

It wasn't what had actually occurred.

"I'll arrange a paternity test if you want," Cory offered, her voice quiet. She'd changed from how he remembered her in his mind. Her dark hair was shorter, just skimming her shoulders. Her slim build, rosy lips and the sprinkling of freckles across her nose remained the same. But there was something different about her deep brown eyes. They were guarded now and looked world-weary, as if she'd seen things and experienced feelings that changed her at a cellular level. Somehow it made her even more appealing.

He'd barely been able to speak after she dropped

that bombshell on the sidewalk. A part of him, the shadowy fragment that never planned to become a father, had urged him to send her away.

Jordan had a good life in Starlight. He liked the town and the people living in it. He liked owning a local watering hole and had worked hard to elevate Trophy Room from a dumpy dive bar to a popular hangout for locals and visitors alike. His existence was simple and straightforward, and he worked hard to keep it that way.

Cory Hall was ten kinds of complicated. That was without a baby thrown into the mix.

Jordan didn't want complications.

Instead of sending her away, he'd told her to bring the baby into the bar. He'd unlocked the door, flipped on the light and reentered the space he knew like the back of his hand.

With Cory following close on his heels, he saw the bar through her eyes. Through the lens of someone who'd known him when he was a big deal in the world, or at least had a monster-size attitude. He'd changed, and because of that, he couldn't send her away without at least hearing her out.

Then the baby, who'd been sleeping soundly in the car-seat contraption Cory carried him in, had woken. She'd quickly made a bottle while Jordan stared out the bar's front window into the peaceful night and said a fond farewell to the calm he'd known in life.

"He looks just like me," he said through clenched teeth.

"Yeah." Cory smiled down at the baby, who was beginning to drift off once again. "He has your eyes. I've never seen eyes that color on anyone else."

"They're my father's eyes," Jordan said, then clamped his mouth shut. He wasn't going to bring his dad into this conversation. "Why didn't you reach out to me right away, Cory? I can't believe I'm just finding out about him."

"I'm sorry." Her delicate brows drew together. "I was reeling after you left Atlanta. I thought…" Heat crept into her cheeks, and she shook her head. "It doesn't matter what I thought."

"You went back to Kade."

"Not right away. We gave it another try after I found out I was pregnant," she admitted. "It seemed like the best thing for the baby. I had a few complications at the start of the pregnancy. When the doctor did the early ultrasound, I realized that, based on the date of conception, the baby wasn't Kade's."

"And there was no one else other than me?"

She closed her eyes for a moment, and he could see how much the question hurt her. Damn it. Even now, he didn't want to hurt her.

"Forget I asked that," he said, lowering himself into a chair across from her. "I know this baby is mine. Did you tell Kade?"

Her mouth tightened. "I told him I'd been with

someone else during our breakup. He wanted me to give him a name, but I wouldn't."

"And he just let you go?"

"That's not exactly how I'd describe it. He kicked me out of the house with nothing but the clothes on my back. I stayed with a friend for a couple of days and managed to get one of the other guys' girlfriends to help me retrieve some of my belongings. But most of what I had, he'd bought for me. The clothes, the car, the jewelry."

"Did those things mean a lot to you?"

She rolled her eyes. "I'm pretty sure you know they didn't. I never cared about that stuff."

"I thought I knew you," he said quietly, the ache in his chest expanding with every moment that passed. "But now I wonder. The woman I knew wouldn't have kept a baby from me."

"I get it." She adjusted her hold on the child, cradling him more snugly against her. "With how you left, I was afraid you wouldn't want anything to do with me, and it would have broken my heart. I'd planned to contact you after he was born, but with the surgery and follow-up visits, there was so much happening."

"What surgery?" Jordan sat straighter in the heavy oak chair.

"Ben had a congenital heart defect. The doctors discovered it shortly after he was born," she explained. "He had surgery when he was five days old."

"What kind of defect?" Jordan demanded, then took in a calming breath when the baby startled. "Sorry, I didn't mean to shout."

"It's okay." Cory gave him a hesitant smile. The smiles he remembered from her had been wide and beaming, like she was a character in that old TV show his grandma used to watch, turning the world on with her smile. "It was a narrowing of the aorta, and his lower extremities weren't getting enough blood flow, so they had to do surgery to correct it. It was scary, but he came through like a champ. According to the pediatric cardiologist, he's healthy now. And he's perfect." He watched as she drew in a shuddery breath and then added, "To me, he's perfect."

Jordan pressed two fingers to his chest in an attempt to rub away the deep ache that surfaced at the obvious love in her voice. Questions and accusations surged through him in angry waves. He had a child. His baby had been through something as significant as heart surgery, and he hadn't been there. He'd had no idea. "You dealt with all that on your own?"

Cory shook her head. "I went back to Michigan and moved in with my grandma. Mom didn't want much to do with me. She was too mad that I'd thrown away my 'meal ticket.'" It was clear by the sharp air quotes she made what Cory thought of her mother's opinion.

Jordan agreed. Despite his frustration, Jordan had

to admit it said a lot about her character. He'd had his doubts about that part when he'd left Atlanta. Somehow the knowledge that he hadn't been wrong about her priorities softened the sharp edge of anger he seemed to be skating at the moment.

"Gran was great, but…" Her gaze went dark. "She passed away last month."

"I'm sorry," he said automatically.

"I was happy to be with her at the end, and I'm grateful she got to meet her great-grandson. In fact, Gran was the one who made me promise I'd seek you out to tell you about Ben."

"Thanks, Gran," he said, glancing up at the ceiling.

"I don't expect anything from you." Cory gave a quiet laugh. "Lowering my expectations has become par for the course these days. If you want to be a part of his life—"

"Who do you think I am?" Jordan demanded, temper flaring again. "Hell, yes, I want to be a part of his life, Cory. He's my son. I don't know how we're going to figure this out, but I can guaran-damn-tee you I'm not letting him go."

"Okay," she said. "We'll find a way to make it work. Gran always said everything is figure-outable. I believe that."

She spoke softly, her tone calm, like she was trying to gentle an angry bear. Jordan sighed when he realized he was the bear. Another benefit of his simple life was that it allowed him to stay in control of his emotions. When he didn't feel much of anything, he couldn't get himself into trouble.

Tonight a bomb had gone off, blowing apart the simple life he'd crafted in Starlight. Despite Cory's vow to make it work, he had no doubt his moratorium on trouble had just been lifted.

Chapter Two

Cory woke early the next morning, light just beginning to make its way through the edges of the heavy curtains she'd pulled tight over the window of the inn the night before. She turned on her side to watch Ben asleep in the crib the inn's owner had helped her set up when they'd arrived yesterday afternoon.

She'd shared a bedroom with her son since the day she finally brought him home from the hospital, almost a full week after he was born. Last night, she'd explained the baby's heart condition to Jordan with the calm of hindsight, but there was no way to describe the terror she'd felt watching her newborn being taken to the operating room in that sterile hospital.

She wasn't sure if she'd ever adequately be able to communicate all the reasons she'd taken so long to reach out to Jordan and tell him he had a son. He'd been angry and shocked, both of which she'd expected, but he'd also been surprisingly quick to commit to being a part of Ben's life.

Cory didn't have much experience with men and commitment. Her own father had left town when Cory was barely a toddler, and she'd had virtually no relationship with him since then. She'd thought Kade, whom she'd met her sophomore and his senior year at the University of Michigan, was committed to their relationship. He'd certainly demanded her devotion, begging her to leave school early when he was drafted. Despite her doubts, she'd done what he asked and believed him when he told her she could transfer to a different college once they were settled.

Then she'd been swept into the world of being a full-time girlfriend, always available to cater to Kade's never-ending list of needs.

She'd worked at a small boutique owned by one of the coaches' wives and tried to ignore the fact that every aspect of her life was set up to revolve around a man. It shamed her to think about how much of herself she'd given away in those years. When she'd driven away from Atlanta, hand on her belly like she could draw strength from the life growing inside her, she'd promised herself she would never give away her power or conform to a man's desires in lieu of her own dreams.

Now she was in a strange bed in a strange town, unsure of what the future held because she was waiting for a man to decide what he wanted from her. Her gut tightened painfully as a familiar wave of regret rolled over her.

The unexpected friendship with Jordan had been a bright spot in her life. Because he was a veteran player with an impeccable reputation, team management had asked him to mentor Kade on his behavior, both on and off the field. Jordan made an effort, but Kade didn't like to be told what to do. Still, Jordan became a regular part of their lives.

For Cory, who always felt alone despite being constantly surrounded by people, Jordan's easygoing charm and lack of interest in the postseason party scene held a powerful appeal. They'd talked for hours and fallen into an easy rhythm of sharing parts of themselves that no one else saw. She'd come to depend on his steady presence, and when things fell apart after their one night together, it had been a huge loss.

What would they be to each other going forward? She couldn't imagine a way back to the connection they'd once had. For all she knew, based on how he'd left Atlanta without a word to her, all of those feelings had been one-sided anyway.

She and Jordan hadn't discussed next steps last night. In truth, Cory had been so exhausted from a mix of the adrenaline crash and plain old fatigue that she wasn't sure she would have lasted through another heated conversation. Ben had saved her from having to admit how overwhelmed she was by fussing enough that she knew she needed to get him to bed.

They'd exchanged numbers and agreed to meet today to make a plan. Cory reminded herself that she wasn't waiting for Jordan to call the shots.

Gran might not have had anything but the Buick to leave her, but she could start over and make her way in the world however she saw fit. Cory had spent most of the months after Ben's recovery nursing her grandmother until the cancer stole Gran's life. Despite the lingering guilt at keeping father and son apart for a time, she would fight for whatever she deemed best.

Unfortunately for her, she had no money, no home and very few prospects to provide for her son on her own. Gran had left her the car, but Cory's mother had taken everything else.

Determination. She had a soul-deep determination to give her baby a good life. However that unfolded, Cory would make it work. Of course, it would be a lot easier if Jordan had gone bald or ended up with a beer belly in the time since she'd last seen him.

They'd spent only one night together, but her body still seemed to be tuned to his like some kind of powerful radio frequency. The last thing she needed was to be distracted by her son's father.

She continued to watch Ben sleep, his little chest rising and falling in steady breaths. Not a day went by that she didn't think about what he'd been through and the gift she'd been given when he recovered from the surgery.

Cory might not have much now, but she could imagine what the future would bring if she continued to work toward her goal of providing a good life for him. She saw him as a toddler and then a young boy, playing in a backyard with green grass and pretty potted flowers. Maybe they'd adopt a puppy one day, a furry beastie that would love Ben best of all, just the way she did.

She quietly showered and got dressed, an expert at getting ready in silence so as not to disturb him. When he woke an hour later and gave her a radiant smile, her heart filled with hope and her eyes with tears. She would do anything to ensure her child had a better, happier childhood than hers. Not a high bar to surpass, but one she planned to leapfrog just the same.

She changed his diaper, fed him a bottle and a bit of rice cereal, then changed him from pajamas into one of her favorite outfits—a striped shirt under tiny overalls. He was her little man, and she believed without reservation that he was the cutest baby ever. Most moms probably felt that way, but it was important to Cory that Jordan also recognize it.

He hadn't even held Ben last night, and she'd been

too nervous to push the issue. As he'd walked her to her car after they agreed to meet today, he'd reached out and traced a finger along Ben's temple. She'd heard his sharp intake of breath, like the touch had sparked him in some way.

There'd been no text from Jordan this morning, and she wondered if he was a late sleeper because of long nights at the bar. She figured she'd get coffee and a pastry at the coffee shop she'd passed in town and then call him once she was fortified with caffeine and a hefty dose of sugar.

Ben had been crying when they'd arrived back at the hotel last night, so she'd left the infant seat in the car and carried him in her arms to their room.

Instead of waiting for the elevator, she took the stairs to the lobby. The inn's lot had been relatively empty both times she'd parked. She guessed a weeknight in late March wasn't a popular time for tourists.

If she'd done the math right, she had two more nights to stay at the hotel before she maxed out her remaining credit card. Hopefully today's conversation with Jordan would help clarify next steps. She hadn't really thought beyond carrying out her gran's request. Cory had gotten used to taking things one day at a time, especially in the last weeks of her grandmother's battle with cancer.

It was time to start planning for her future and to figure out what role a sexy, grumpy, definitely off-limits man might play in it.

She exited the heavy door that led to the lobby and stopped in her tracks, her heart beginning to beat an uneven clip in her chest.

As if she'd conjured him with her unwelcome thoughts, Jordan sat in one of the cozy space's overstuffed armchairs, clearly waiting for her. And not looking the least bit happy about it.

"Do you actually think I would have skipped town?" Cory gave Jordan a sidelong glare as he maneuvered the hulking SUV he drove along the winding mountain road that apparently led to his house. "I sought you out in the first place."

"Because your grandma made you promise," he reminded her. "I'm guessing you didn't think I'd want to be part of my son's life."

She chewed on her bottom lip. "I didn't not think you would."

He snorted.

"The past few months haven't exactly been a cakewalk for me," she said, trying not to sound as overwhelmed as she felt. "Of course I hoped you'd want to get to know Ben. I want my child to grow up with a father in his life."

"Our child," Jordan corrected.

"Ours." She nodded. "You have my phone number. Why didn't you just call to make plans?"

"I wasn't sure you'd answer," he said, and she appreciated his honesty. "As I remember, you weren't great with the follow-up."

Annoyance burned her stomach like someone had dumped a bottle of acid down her throat. She knew he was referring to the one night they'd spent together, when she'd left his bed early the next morning before he woke up.

At that point, Cory had thought she was done with Kade, and to fall for another guy—let alone another football player—went against everything she'd thought she wanted for herself.

It didn't matter that Jordan was completely different from Kade, both in how he approached his career and how he treated her. She ignored the fact that he seemed to want to be her friend as well as her lover. Cory had been too raw from the breakup and unwilling to trust her heart again.

By the time she'd gotten up the nerve to go to his condo later that week, he'd moved out and moved on. His Atlanta number had been disconnected, and she'd taken that as a fairly concrete sign that he had no inclination to hear from her.

"As I remember, you cut and ran pretty quickly when things weren't easy to manage." She glanced into the back seat and smiled at Ben, who laughed, kicked his feet and then went back to staring out the window at the pine trees flanking either side of the road. "A baby isn't easy, Jordan."

"I understand," he said quietly. "I googled his surgery when I got home last night. He went through a lot for such a little guy."

"The hardest thing I've ever had to deal with was knowing I had no power to take away his pain."

"I'm sure you did everything you could to make sure he got through it."

She shrugged. "The doctors and nurses had more to do with that than me. All I did was spend those hours in a hospital waiting room, wondering if he'd survive and what I'd done wrong that he'd been born with that sort of complication."

Jordan's fingers tightened on the steering wheel. "It was a congenital defect. That had nothing to do with you."

"Mom guilt is a powerful thing." She laughed without humor. "You'd be amazed at the dark paths where the mind of a mom can wander."

"Did your mom ever feel guilty about the way she raised you?"

Cory shook her head. "She was too busy trying to land another boyfriend or husband to spend much time thinking about me. I'm guessing your mom didn't have much time for guilt, either." She glanced out the window. She and Jordan had shared a lot about each other's childhoods during the football season when they became friends.

"She was too busy keeping my dad happy," he answered without emotion.

They fell into a silence that should have been

awkward. Cory guessed he was as entrenched in unwelcome childhood memories as she was. She certainly had a treasure trove from which to choose. Her mom had made it clear over and over that Cory had changed everything about her life, and not for the better. Cory had done her best not to be a burden and had learned from an early age how to make herself smaller so her mom—and later her boyfriends— wouldn't have to deal with the weight of her love.

Her stomach churned at the thought of how she'd lost herself trying to be what other people wanted— or maybe she'd never been found in the first place. Jordan's fingers were tight on the steering wheel, and she wondered what dark path his mind was traveling along.

The air seemed to hold a thousand unspoken regrets, but it wasn't uncomfortable in the quiet of the car, the thick forests of the Pacific Northwest surrounding them. For the first time since she'd found out about the pregnancy, Cory felt a sliver of peace doing its best to bloom inside her heart.

Maybe because no matter what kind of arrangement she and Jordan made, at least she knew she was no longer alone in raising her child.

"I want to be a good mom," she said as he turned onto a narrow driveway. "I don't want to make him feel the way I felt as a kid. Like I was an inconvenience that held her back from the life she wanted.

Even if she didn't say it out loud, I always understood I was the root of the problems in her life."

Jordan slowed as he steered the SUV up the winding gravel drive. "You won't do that."

"How do you know?" She knew she sounded weak, needing confirmation, but she couldn't stand the thought that she might fall into the same pattern as her mother. Although Gran and Mom had been estranged for the better part of Cory's life, her grandmother hadn't once spoken an ill word about her difficult daughter.

"She did her best" was all she would ever say. Cory didn't want to believe that her mom had tried her best at parenting, because that might mean Cory could do her best and still end up hurting Ben. The thought terrified her more than she could explain.

"I just know," Jordan said as he pulled to a stop.

Well, that wasn't very reassuring. Then her gaze switched from him to the truck's front window. She'd been so focused on watching Jordan, searching his face for confirmation as to whether he was telling her the truth or blowing sunshine up her proverbial skirt, that she hadn't noticed the house.

It was magnificent, a two-story log cabin with an expansive wraparound deck, large windows and a burnished slate roof that made the cabin look like it had been in these woods for generations.

"Wow," she murmured. "The bartending business must be treating you right."

He chuckled. "More like the NFL retirement business after having my knee blown out on national television."

She tore her gaze from the house and focused on him again. "I'm sorry that happened to you."

"Not your fault," he said and climbed out of the vehicle.

She exited and then unhooked Ben's infant seat and lifted it out, as well.

"I can take it," Jordan said as he came to stand a few feet away.

Some tiny part of her resisted handing the carrier over to him, which was ridiculous. She'd sought out her baby's father. Of course he'd want to hold the boy.

"Thanks." She gave Jordan the carrier, and he hooked an arm under the handle, then headed for the house.

"Did you have to do a lot of work on this place when you moved in?"

He shook his head. "I bought it from a Seattle couple who'd used it as a weekend retreat. They'd totally remodeled the interior, although I added an outdoor living area in back."

"Divorce?" she guessed.

"After twenty years," he confirmed. "It was sad, actually, although I got lucky with the property."

"I wonder if the statistic that people throw around about fifty percent of marriages ending in divorce is accurate. Sometimes it seems like it should be higher.

Can you imagine being with someone for two decades and then walking away?"

He shrugged. "Some people stay married even when divorce is a better option."

Was he talking about his own parents? She knew he'd had a difficult relationship with his father, which had led to challenges with his mom due to her loyalty to her husband.

"I heard a rumor Kade is getting married," she said, then wished she'd kept her mouth shut.

Jordan's gaze cut to hers. "Does that bother you?"

"No. He called a bunch after I left Atlanta, trying to convince me to come back, and…" She shook her head as she thought about what her ex-boyfriend had suggested she do to handle the pregnancy. "It doesn't matter. I didn't want to return to that life or raise a child in the midst of it."

Jordan didn't say anything in response as he opened the front door and then stepped aside to let her enter first.

"No lock?"

One corner of his mouth lifted into a smirk. "I'm too far out of town for locks. Actually, I'm not sure if anyone in Starlight locks their doors. It's the kind of town where a person feels safe."

Cory had trouble imagining a world where she'd feel safe. Safe from heartache, disappointment and the constant worry about providing a good life for her son. But she was more than ready to try.

Chapter Three

Jordan filled two glasses with water and tamped down the maelstrom of emotion surging through his veins. He glanced over his shoulder to see Cory lifting the baby—his baby—over her head. She grinned and cooed sweet words, bringing Ben close enough to shower him with kisses and then lifting him again.

The boy loved the game, laughing and waving his arms before curling his chubby fingers into his mother's hickory-colored hair.

She'd been beautiful when he first met her in Atlanta. One glance at her soft caramel-colored eyes and that sweet smile, and he'd lost a bit of his hardened heart. She seemed more herself now in a casual sweatshirt and faded jeans with no makeup and her hair holding a bit of natural curl. But to witness her so filled with love for her child took his reaction to a whole new level.

One that wasn't smart for either of them.

He'd told himself his night with Cory had been a fling, although somewhere deep inside he knew that was a lie. But it had been easier than admitting he'd fallen for a woman he had no right to want.

She clearly hadn't wanted anything to do with him after sneaking out of his bed the morning after. He might not be the sharpest knife in the drawer, but she'd given him a pretty straightforward hint as to what being with him meant to her.

Jordan's plan had been to leave Atlanta when his lease ended. He'd known his injury would end his career. It said something about his commitment that after seven seasons with the same team, he was still renting a basic condo near downtown instead of buying a place of his own. So it was easy to move up the time frame for leaving. His injury during the playoff game that season signaled the end to his NFL career, which he hadn't found as upsetting as he probably should have.

By the time he got to that point, he'd lost much of his love of the game. It had simply become a job for him, and since Jordan didn't care for the trappings of pro-athlete fame, it hadn't been hard to walk away from his career and start over. He'd returned to Washington but come to Starlight because he liked the small-town feel and the bar was an easy business to manage. Jordan discovered that after so many years of pushing himself, he appreciated ease.

Forgetting Cory had been anything but easy.

He'd managed eventually—or so he'd thought—but now here she was, sitting on his leather couch, looking like she belonged in his world. He didn't want to admit how much he liked seeing her in his space, how her reaction to the unique beauty of his home had made his chest ache with yearning.

She was there because they needed to work out plans for raising a child together. Nothing more.

Sleep had been elusive last night. Jordan had spent hours combing the internet to learn the specifics about Ben's surgery. He'd finally drifted off only to wake in a cold sweat an hour later, panic gripping at the thought that Cory might change her mind and leave town.

He would have tracked her down, of course. She might not expect much from the men in her life, but Jordan would never shirk his parental responsibility, even though he didn't know the first thing about being a father.

The only certainty was that he would do it differently than his own father had. Looking into Ben's eyes—his gaze both familiar and not—had upended Jordan's world. He'd never intended to start a family of his own, but he would do his best no matter what.

"He's happy this morning." Jordan placed the

two waters on the coffee table and started to take a seat in one of the chairs across from the sofa. He'd hosted the bar's holiday party at his house last year but otherwise hadn't had many visitors to his home. It hadn't felt lonely before. He liked the solitude. But he had the feeling he'd notice the silence in a different way once Cory and the baby went back to town.

"Do you want to hold him?" she asked, her gaze both expectant and hopeful.

"I might break him," Jordan answered automatically, but he straightened and took a step closer, heart thudding dully.

"You'll do fine." She shifted on the sofa to make room and then reached out and tugged on his hand. The gentle touch made Jordan's lungs squeeze as he remembered how soft Cory's skin was—everywhere.

Keeping his features steady so she didn't realize her effect on him, he sat down next to her. She transferred Ben to his arms, and he felt the baby tense slightly, like he was unsure about being handed off to a stranger.

Jordan didn't blame the kid, but he also hated the thought that he was a stranger to his own child. The reminder that he'd been robbed of the first six months with his boy was the splash of cold water his heart needed to go icy again.

"Relax," Cory urged in her sweet voice. "He's an easy baby. Last night he was overtired, which is why he fussed so much. Normally he has a sunny attitude."

"Are you a ray of sunshine?" Jordan asked, amazed at how solid such a small creature felt in his arms. Ben's green gaze locked on Jordan's as his mouth widened into a toothless grin.

Jordan held the baby's torso and turned him. Ben planted his feet on Jordan's denim-clad legs and bounced up and down, smiling the entire time.

"He's really active, too," Cory said with a laugh. She rose from the sofa. "Shoot. I left the diaper bag in your truck. His toys and a blanket are in there. We can put him on the floor to play while we talk."

"Wait. You aren't leaving me alone with him." So much for steady. Even Jordan recognized the panic in his own voice.

"Only for a minute." She patted his shoulder as she moved past him. "You'll be fine."

Jordan wasn't convinced, but arguing would make him sound like a complete wussy. He'd faced off against the toughest defensemen the NFL had to offer, so why was he terrified of one small baby?

"Don't cry," he told the child, who shoved a fist into his mouth in response. "Please."

To his great relief, Ben seemed content to bob up and down and stare at Jordan.

"I like to see you starting squats early," Jordan told him when he finally started to relax. "They're important for overall leg strength. You might want to give it a rest on chewing your own hand. I'm not sure if you realize it, but the sleeve of your shirt is already soaked in drool."

"He's teething," Cory explained as she returned.

"That diaper bag–retrieval mission took five hours," Jordan stated. "But Ben and I managed just fine, so you know."

She laughed again. "You're a natural."

Hardly, based on the relief he felt when she took the baby from him. She placed him on his back on the colorful fleece blanket she'd spread across the rug and handed him a plastic telephone that played obnoxious, tinny music.

"Have you introduced him to Luke Bryan?" Jordan asked as she sat next to him.

Her brows drew together. "Not officially, although we listened to a lot of country stations on the drive out here."

Jordan nodded. "Music is important. He needs to know the classics of country, rock and blues. Also how to swing a bat the right way and how to change a tire. I see too many kids around town who don't know the first thing about car maintenance. It's a sad turn of events."

"Whoa, there." Cory held up a hand. "He's six months old. Right now we're working on solid foods. Car mechanics come a bit down the road."

"Right." Jordan scrubbed a hand over his jaw. "But I'm going to be there for all of it. I want to be clear on that, Cory. Ben is my son, and I'm going to be a part of his life forever."

Cory wasn't sure how to describe the riot of feelings that comprised her response to Jordan's declaration. Her body's response to him. A day of stubble darkened his jaw, and the laugh lines around his green eyes captivated her. Everything about him appealed to her, and that was not good. Of course, his willingness to step up as a parent was what she wanted for her son—a father who would be there for every phase of his life.

When she'd made the promise to her grandmother that she'd introduce Ben to his father, she hadn't thought about what it would mean for her own life. Yes, it was a relief to think about having a partner in parenting, but having Jordan involved also meant she'd be relinquishing control. It meant that Ben would spend time with his dad away from her. There would be custody arrangements and co-parenting challenges.

She might be giving up as much as she was gaining.

The thought didn't sit well.

At the same time, she was humbled by Jordan's immediate acceptance of the situation and the sincerity of his commitment. There was no doubt in her mind that he'd be a great father. He had financial security, owned his own business and lived in a town that was just about picture-perfect.

Cory had her gran's old Buick and a trunk full of everything she owned in the world. No college degree, no career to speak of and not one friend she could call for moral support.

The idea her son could grow up to be disappointed by her strengthened her resolve to make something of her life. She refused to go down the same path her mom had traveled, constantly scrambling and struggling to make her romantic relationships work. Her mom had terrible taste in men. She picked boyfriends who were selfish and treated her like an afterthought.

Cory thought about everything she'd done to fit into Kade's world. She'd wanted him to love her in the same way he loved football and the fame that came with it. But that was never going to happen, and she wished she'd accepted the truth long before she did. She felt a bone-deep commitment to protecting her heart going forward so she'd have more of it to give to Ben.

"I'm here so you can be a part of his life," Cory said, relieved when her voice didn't tremble. "I want you to have a relationship with him, Jordan. The next step is to figure out how that's going to work for all of us."

Jordan nodded and looked at her in a way that had awareness zinging along her nerve endings. The weight of his gaze seemed to hold the promise of what might have been. "I don't mean how you and I will work," she clarified. "There's no you and I, of course."

"Of course," he murmured in that rumbly tone. "Also, I assume you're planning to stay in Starlight. This is my home and I want Ben close."

Her first instinct was to argue, because somehow the assumption grated at her. With the few details she'd given him about her life since he'd left Atlanta, Jordan didn't know that she was basically on her own and homeless with little savings and fewer prospects back in Michigan.

She'd told him about the promise to Gran, and he knew about her strained relationship with her mom. But that was it. As far as he was concerned, Cory had a great life in Michigan. Her grandmother might have left her a secret fortune in the old car's glove box.

Never mind none of that was anywhere near the truth.

Before she could answer, the shrill ring of his cell phone sounded from the kitchen counter. Ben moved his head in the direction of the noise, overly loud in the silence that had settled in the house.

"Let me check who it is." Jordan stood and stepped over the baby's blanket, easy with his long legs. Cory did her best not to notice how the faded denim conformed to the muscles of his thighs. She almost smiled as she thought of the fact that tight end, his football position, was the perfect description of the man himself.

She got up off the couch and went to sit on the floor next to Ben, surreptitiously watching Jordan's reaction to whoever was on the other end of the line. He sent the call to voice mail, and the phone almost immediately began to ring again.

He hit the mute button and then quickly punched in and sent a text. A moment later the phone dinged with a response, and he frowned at the screen, his thick brows drawn together.

"Persistent girlfriend?" she asked, trying to sound casual when he returned to the family room.

"My mother," he said tightly.

"Is everything okay?"

He shrugged. "I have to make a quick trip to my hometown tomorrow morning. Family function. I'll be gone for a couple of days."

"Okay." She nodded, unsure what to make of his darkening mood. "I have the hotel room booked for another night. After that, I need to figure out where to—"

"You should go with me," he said suddenly.

Cory blinked. "To your family function?"

"Yeah." Jordan nodded as if he was working out the details in his mind. "I grew up outside Spokane. It's about two hours from here. If we leave around eight—"

"I haven't agreed to anything," Cory protested.

"Even if I was willing to go with you, won't your family think it's odd?" She smoothed a hand over Ben's soft forehead. "You were the one who said he has your father's eyes. Your dad might be a bit shocked when you show up with a baby who looks like him."

"My dad won't be shocked," Jordan answered, his tone frigid enough to freeze water. "I haven't seen anyone in my family since I moved back to Washington. They don't know a thing about my current life, other than I own a bar in a town they have no intention of visiting. This is actually perfect. You and Ben come with me, and that will distract everyone. They'll be too busy focusing on the baby to remind me how badly I screwed up my life by having the stupid luck to be injured in that game."

"They can't blame you for the injury," Cory told him, her brain firing on a dozen cylinders. There were things Jordan wasn't telling her about his relationship with his family and what this trip meant. Despite her reservations, she didn't like the thought of anyone trying to make him feel guilty for something he had no control over. She'd dealt with plenty of that in her life, and it was awful.

"Please come with me." He closed his eyes for a moment, then opened them again, and the pain she saw in their depths sliced across her heart.

His eyes were so similar to her baby's, and she hated the thought that anything would ever cause

Ben to look that way. "This situation is complicated, which isn't exactly my comfort zone. It might be helpful if we could spend a couple of days getting to know each other again before we make any definite decisions about the plan for going forward. You can think about whether you want to stay in Starlight."

He offered a tentative smile. "I hope you decide you will. I can't imagine a better place to raise a child."

"Do you have a girlfriend?" she blurted, then pulled her bottom lip between her teeth. It was none of her business, but the thought of Jordan raising children with some gorgeous mountain woman made an unwelcome pit of jealousy open in her stomach.

He frowned and shook his head. "Do you have a boyfriend?"

She rolled her eyes. "I barely have time to brush my teeth. Men are way too much work for me right now."

"Good to know." He drew in a deep breath, his chest rising and falling under the flannel shirt. "Will you go with me, Cory? You and Ben. I promise I'll make sure you have time for teeth brushing while we're away."

That simple vow made her smile. It was ludicrous to agree to it. She and Jordan needed to come up with a custody agreement, not get to know each other. But for the first time in as long as she could remember, Cory didn't feel the heavy weight of stress and responsibility. Her life wasn't much to speak of at the moment. What would be the harm in delaying decisions about the future for a few days? She could attend whatever wedding or family reunion he had to make an appearance at, and it might even be fun. At least there would probably be lots of free food.

"Do you want to go on a road trip with your daddy?" She lifted her son into her arms and cradled him close. Ben made a high-pitched squealing sound.

"Sounded like a yes to me," Jordan told her.

"Okay," she said. "We can work out plans for co-parenting on the drive."

"Whatever you want."

"I left most of my nice clothes in Atlanta," she told him, trying not to sound bitter. "So my wardrobe choices are limited. If it's a fancy wedding—"

"It's not." Jordan turned to gaze out the picture window that overlooked the pond behind his house and then back to her. "It's a funeral. My father's funeral."

Chapter Four

Jordan winced as a bony elbow jabbed him in the ribs later that night. "Hey," he protested. "Unnecessary roughness."

Tanya Mehall, Trophy Room's primary bartender, arched a brow as she turned her back on the customers sitting at the bar to face him. "You're scaring people with tonight's perma-scowl," she said in a low voice. "I've got enough to handle with the attitude coming from the kitchen. You need to fix your face."

Before he could answer, she lifted a hand and patted his cheek. "Let's see those dimples, boss," she commanded, then moved around him to pour a round of pints for a group near the end of the well-worn mahogany bar.

Tanya was a Starlight native, a few years older than Jordan. From all accounts, she'd spent her teen years babysitting almost every kid in town. Although she remained single, she liked mothering people—customers and coworkers alike.

But she was wrong about Jordan. He didn't scare people, not anymore. A quick glance around the bar's crowded interior had him swallowing back a sigh. The regulars facing him seemed to be collectively attempting not to make eye contact, like they were nervous about how he might react if they had the audacity to meet his gaze.

Damn. He needed to fix his face.

Drawing in a deep breath, he forced a smile and stepped forward. It only took a few minutes of small talk for the line of customers to visibly relax. They discussed the game broadcasting from the television hanging behind the bar, and Jordan made a point to ask Ray Monning about his new grandchild, a girl who had been born the previous week.

That launched his crew of regulars into a heated discussion about whether girls or boys were tougher to raise. Jordan found himself listening with more interest than usual. He wondered in what ways Ben would challenge him. His son. Of course, he didn't mention the bombshell that had been dropped into his lap the previous night, although people around town would learn about it soon enough, especially if he convinced Cory to stay.

He had to convince her to stay. Jordan might still be reeling at the thought of being a father, but that didn't mean he wasn't committed to figuring out how to manage it.

He'd already ordered a half dozen books on parenting and had spent most of the afternoon watching instructional online videos on everything from diaper changing to developmental milestones. He was going to get this right on some level.

Nick Dunlap, Starlight's police chief, appeared at the far end of the bar and lifted a hand to wave at Jordan, who nodded in response. It was Thursday, which meant Nick was picking up dinner for his fiancée, Brynn, and her son, Tyler. With a ten-year-old boy and a baby daughter at home, the couple rarely spent much time in the bar, but Brynn was a bit addicted to the Trophy Room wings, which Jordan appreciated.

"I'm going to grab Nick's food," Jordan told Tanya as he headed for the kitchen.

"Keep smiling and tell Madison not to make anyone else cry tonight."

"Someone cried?" Jordan asked automatically, then shook his head. "Do I want to know?"

"Probably not. Smile," Tanya repeated.

Simple, Jordan told himself as he entered the bar's refurbished kitchen. He could keep his life simple and his emotions on an even keel, despite the changes.

"Are you having a good night?" he asked Colleen,

one of the servers, as she placed plates on a large serving tray.

She glanced up at him, then over her shoulder, and rolled her eyes. "Sure," she said, sounding totally unconvincing.

"Her customers would have a better night if she could get the lead out," a feminine voice said from behind the industrial range positioned on the far side of the kitchen. "No one wants lukewarm burgers."

Colleen flashed a patently fake smile. "That's my cue." She moved past Jordan, muttering under her breath as she went.

"No one is complaining." He walked forward until he faced his surly chef, then flinched as Madison Maurer fixed him with a glare that could sear a rib eye. He'd hired the edgy blonde chef despite her spotty résumé. There were periods of unemployment, and she readily admitted she'd left at least one former job because she didn't get along with the restaurant's owner.

But the caliber of kitchen she'd cooked in throughout the Pacific Northwest was stellar, and she had five-star reviews to spare. He hadn't delved into why she wanted a job running a bar kitchen, but he was glad she had. With her skill and creativity, Madison had improved Trophy Room's menu. Unfortunately, they were going to run out of potential servers for that food if she continued to scare off his staff.

"Because people in this town are too nice." Madison Maurer gave an order to one of the kitchen workers, then stepped closer to Jordan. "That doesn't excuse lack of effort."

"Colleen makes an effort," Jordan countered. "Everyone on staff does. We should make sure we appreciate and recognize that effort."

Madison narrowed her icy blue eyes at him. "Tanya got to you."

He crossed his arms over his chest. "Did you make someone cry?"

"Not exactly."

Danny, one of the line cooks, poked his head around the fryer. "She told that new waitress you hired she was a waste of space."

Jordan groaned. "Where is Samantha now?"

"She quit," Danny offered. "That's why Colleen is so frazzled."

"Everyone knows you have to have thick skin to work in the restaurant industry," Madi grumbled. "I did you a favor."

"Not so much," Jordan said, shaking his head. "Right now I need Nick's food. I'm heading out for a couple of days tomorrow. We'll discuss this in more detail when I get back."

Madison's full mouth pressed into a thin line as she handed him a large brown paper bag. "I don't think there's anything to talk about. I put extra sauce in the bag because Brynn likes her wings wet."

"We'll discuss your opinion, as well," Jordan told her. "Thanks for taking care of Brynn."

"See." Madi held up her hands, palms out. "I'm all about customer service."

Danny let out a loud cackle.

Jordan smiled tightly but didn't answer his surly chef. There was no denying that hiring Madison Maurer was one of the best things he'd done to elevate Trophy Room from a standard bar to the gastropub he envisioned. But to say she was prickly made a cactus seem as soft as a kitten.

Normally, Jordan took a hands-off approach to managing his staff. He hired good people and stayed out of their way so they could do the job. But if he couldn't hold on to staff because Madison chased them away with her bad attitude, that was a problem.

Add it to the list.

He handed the bag to Nick and mentioned the extra wing sauce.

"Brynn will be thrilled," the police chief confirmed with a smile. "You okay, Schaeffer?"

"Yeah. Peachy keen." Seriously, what was wrong with Jordan that everyone could read his emotions so easily?

"Nice crowd for a Thursday," Nick commented, still studying him.

"It's the food, without a doubt."

"No one can resist Madi's wings and sliders."

"She's got skills, that's for sure."

"If you need anything, man, reach out. Okay?"

"I'll do that," Jordan said, a bit of the tension in his chest loosening. He appreciated the reminder he wasn't alone in facing the sudden complications of his life. He mainly kept to himself when he wasn't working, but as a bar and restaurant owner, Jordan had gotten to know a lot of people in town. Good people. Caring people. People who would help build a community around his son.

"How's Remi?" he asked just as Nick turned for the door.

The police chief grinned. "Sweeter by the day. She's almost sitting up on her own. We're hoping the adoption is finalized in the next couple of months."

Jordan leaned forward. "You made it seem so effortless, the instant family deal."

Just before Christmas last year, Nick and Brynn had taken in an abandoned baby, the child of Brynn's late husband and the man's mistress. The way Jordan understood it, Nick and Brynn had been close friends growing up, but they'd had a falling-out during high school. It had taken the baby to bring them together again, and now Jordan couldn't imagine a happier family.

He also couldn't imagine that kind of future for himself, although becoming a father made him committed to try.

"There's definitely a lot of effort," Nick answered

with a laugh. "But it's worth every moment." He waved over his shoulder as he headed for the door.

Jordan rubbed at his chest, where his heart seemed to beat an unsteady rhythm. Would he ever seem that comfortable with his role as a dad? He wanted to ask Nick how he'd managed instant parenthood, but things were still so tenuous with Cory. Maybe after the trip to Spokane, he'd have a better handle on what came next. Although, deep inside he knew his estranged father's funeral wasn't exactly the ideal place to gain emotional clarity.

A couple approached the bar, and he greeted them with his usual smile. Even that took some effort, but it was his job. He just had to get through the next few days. He could imagine turmoil in his hometown since he'd been estranged from his family for years, but he'd manage it. Then he and Cory could work out their parenting arrangement. Things might feel complicated now, but they didn't have to stay that way. He'd make sure of it.

"Are you sure this isn't going to be weird?" Cory asked the next morning as they drove past a sign that announced they'd enter the town of Spokane in thirty miles.

"I'm counting on it to be weird," Jordan said, shooting her a *duh* glance. "That's what's going to take the attention off my return."

"Oh. Great." Cory swiped her hand across the side

of her mouth. "Now I'm really nervous. Any chance you packed a barf bag?"

"No, but I can pull over if you're going to puke."

"I was joking."

Jordan winked. "Me too. By the way, the dried drool is on the other cheek."

Heat infused Cory's face as she pressed the sleeve of her sweatshirt to her cheek. "I didn't sleep well last night," she told Jordan. "Sorry I wasn't a better driving companion."

"You were fine," he said in that deep, rumbly voice. "Plus, it gave Ben and me time to get acquainted."

Cory huffed out a laugh and glanced into the back seat, where her son was racked out in his car seat.

"Until he dozed off, as well," Jordan admitted, one side of his mouth curving in a way that did funny things to her insides.

"You're quite stimulating," she told him, earning a deep chuckle. She wasn't sure whether the nerves zinging along her spine had more to do with anticipation of meeting Jordan's family or the way he made her feel.

"I'll have to work on that."

"We need to get our story straight," she reminded him.

His smile faded. "It's best not to offer too many details. We met in Atlanta, and now we have Ben."

She turned to face him, adjusting the lap belt as

she shifted. "Your family's not going to question you showing up with a six-month-old baby? Like maybe you would have mentioned it to them prior to now?"

One bulky shoulder lifted and lowered. "I told you we aren't close."

"Your mom not knowing she has a grandchild is a bit more than 'not close,'" Cory felt compelled to point out. "Will she be upset we aren't married?"

"I'm not sure."

Her stomach tightened at his response. "Will she want to have a relationship with Ben after this weekend?"

"Good question."

"I have a million of them where that came from," she said. "I don't even know how your father died."

"Heart attack."

"Sudden." She worried her lower lip between her teeth. There were so many potential potholes for her to tumble into this weekend, and based on the tight set of his jaw, Jordan was in no shape to help her navigate through it. In fact, she had the feeling she'd be the one supporting him and he'd need solace well beyond a distraction.

"Can you answer a question with more than two words?" She was careful to make her voice light and was rewarded when his posture gentled somewhat.

"I suppose so."

"A bonus word. Nice. I'm sorry about your father's death," she said, giving in to the urge to reach out and place her hand on his arm. Of course she should have expected the hard muscles under his jacket. He was a big guy and clearly still in great shape even after his injury and retirement from football. But the touch unsettled her just the same, although she didn't release him. Cory knew what it was like to go through grief alone, and she didn't want that for him. "For your loss."

He said nothing for several moments, and she wondered if she'd already overstepped the bounds of whatever nonrelationship they had.

"It wasn't a loss from my perspective," he said tightly. "We didn't have a relationship."

"Then I'm sorry for that."

He looked at her sharply, like he wanted to rebuke her for the expression of sympathy, but then shook his head. "My mom is sad. She sounds lost, and I don't want that for her. I want her to know how much better off she is without him."

"How long were they married?"

"Thirty-five years."

"And you're thirty, right?" He'd told her his age when they met in Atlanta.

"Yeah."

"Do you have siblings?"

"One brother. Max is twenty-five. My mom had trouble getting pregnant after me, and my parents had long stretches where they weren't exactly close."

She wanted to ask more, but the air was already

so charged. She feared he might shatter as he fought against the emotions she could almost see gripping him. Maybe asking about his brother would defuse some of the tension. "Does he play football?"

Jordan shook his head. "No. He's smart."

Cory wasn't sure whether Jordan meant his brother was smart for not engaging in such a violent sport or was referring to Max's intelligence in some other manner. Either way, she knew it was an implied criticism of himself, and that didn't sit well.

"I think we should stick to the truth as much as we can." She lifted her hand from his arm, immediately missing the warmth that radiated from him like a space heater. "You might not be close to your family, but I'm not looking to cause them more pain or upset by getting caught in a lie. If we simply tell the truth about how we met—"

"A party at your boyfriend's house?" Jordan asked wryly.

"We met in Atlanta during your football career," Cory explained as if he hadn't spoken. She didn't want to revisit those nights of talking to Jordan out by the pool while everyone else partied inside the house. Her time with him had meant more than it should to her.

He'd been kind and sweet, diametrically opposed to how Kade treated her. It had been too easy to fantasize about how different her life might be if she was with someone like Jordan, and even then she'd realized how dangerous that train of thought could be.

Even more now.

"I think we stick with the story that Ben was a surprise—"

"The understatement of the year," Jordan muttered, flipping on his blinker to exit the highway.

Heat crept up Cory's neck, but she ignored it. "But he helped us realize we want to be together. That we're a family."

Her words seemed to reverberate in the silence that followed.

"Sure," Jordan said finally, his voice barely above a whisper. "We'll be in and out for the service so quickly, the details won't really matter."

Cory didn't argue with him, although in her experience, the details always mattered.

"This is a pretty town," she murmured as he turned into a residential neighborhood of modest rows of homes, all with neat yards and fresh paint. "It must have been a big change for you coming to the South after growing up here." She knew that before being drafted to Atlanta, he'd gone to college in Alabama.

"The heat and humidity were hell my first preseason," he admitted with a chuckle. "I must have puked during every practice, but I didn't care. I was so damn happy to be away from here."

"And your dad?"

A stiff nod.

"We'll get through this." It was the mantra Cory had repeated to herself countless times in the past year and a half, but it felt strangely comforting to replace the singular pronoun for the plural *we*. It felt good not to be alone and to be able to offer support instead of being the one who needed it.

She could see Jordan's broad chest rising and falling in shallow breaths and wondered at his reaction. During the football season when they'd been friends, he'd shared enough of his family history that she understood he hadn't remained close with his parents. He'd never mentioned having a brother. His reaction told her he'd left out some of the details of how bad it had been with his dad.

"I've booked two rooms at a hotel downtown," Jordan told her as he pulled to a stop in front of a red-brick rancher with white trim and gutters. "There's no way I'm staying in this house."

"Okay," she answered automatically. This wasn't her homecoming, so she didn't pretend like she had any opinion on how he handled things.

As he turned off the car, she glanced in the back seat to where Ben still napped. Her sweet, handsome boy was about to meet his grandmother.

Cory's mother had only seen the baby twice, and both interactions had been overshadowed by Tracy's disappointment with her daughter. Ben was only a physical reminder of the future Cory had thrown away, according to her mom.

It was silly to pin her hopes on a complete stranger, but Cory hoped Jordan's mom was at least kinder than her own. She couldn't help but want that for her son. A loving family.

She woke Ben and lifted his still-limp body into her arms while Jordan stood next to her, glowering and tapping an agitated toe on the asphalt.

"Do you want to carry him to the house?" she asked as she straightened, the baby cradled against her chest. "It might help relax you a bit."

"I'm relaxed," Jordan countered.

"Like a man about to face the firing squad is relaxed." She offered an encouraging smile. "It's going to be okay, Jordan. You're not alone."

He stared at her like she was speaking a foreign language. "Thanks," he mumbled finally and then smoothed a hand over Ben's downy hair. The boy blinked and lifted his head to study his father, shoving his fist in his mouth.

But Cory noticed that Jordan's shoulders eased ever so slightly and felt a huge sense of accomplishment. She might not know what they were walking into, but she knew how to be useful.

"I'll let you hold him," Jordan said and led them up the narrow walk. "It would be kind of embarrassing if I dropped him or something. To show my mom that I don't even know how to hold my own baby."

"You'll get more comfortable," Cory promised.

The front door opened just before they got to the porch, and an older woman watched from the doorway, hand clasped to her mouth. She was small and delicate, reminding Cory of a fallen leaf that might blow away in a strong gust of wind.

"You came," she whispered as her hazel eyes filled with tears.

"Yeah," Jordan answered simply. "I told you I'd be here." He reached for Cory's elbow and tugged her closer. "I have a couple people for you to meet. My fiancée and my son."

Cory felt her jaw go *clack* and quickly snapped shut her mouth as his mother also tried to hide her shock. Maybe Cory should have pushed for more details from Jordan on the plan, because she wouldn't have guessed in a million years that his suggestion for keeping it simple might involve a fake engagement.

Chapter Five

"A grandson. I still can't believe I have a grandson."

Jordan pressed his lips tight together as he watched his mother smile at the baby she'd been holding in her arms for the past hour.

"It's obvious he likes you," Cory said from where she sat next to Jordan on the pale blue damask sofa in the house's formal living room. Although the home was small, his mother had decorated it with as much pride as if she were holding court at Buckingham Palace. As a kid, Jordan had hated the stuffy decor and the fact he was constantly being told to remove his shoes or to stay out of rooms other than the cozy study off the kitchen.

But his mom had insisted that he and Cory sit with Ben in the once off-limits room at the front of the house. Jordan couldn't help but wonder if he would have been allowed into the precious space if he'd shown up alone.

He swallowed back a yelp when Cory pinched the back of his arm. "Isn't it obvious how much Ben likes his grandma?" she asked.

"He's a baby," Jordan said, earning another squeeze, although her bright smile remained in place. His mother glanced up, and he could clearly see the hope in her gentle gaze. "But, yeah, he likes you, Mom. Of course he does."

"I can't get over how much he looks like your father."

"You mentioned that," Jordan muttered.

"He would have loved to know his grandchild."

Jordan recognized and ignored the soft admonishment.

"If there's anything we can do to help with the service," Cory told his mother, sitting forward, "please know we're here for you."

"Thank you, dear." His mom sniffed. "My book club has handled most of the arrangements. They've been such a help since James passed. I'm not sure how I would have survived without their support."

Jordan fidgeted. Was that a subtle reminder he hadn't been any help to his mom?

He didn't know who was responsible for the distance in their relationship, so he'd always allowed his father to shoulder the blame. His parents' marriage had been tumultuous when Jordan was a kid, but his mom's devotion to her husband never wavered. So when James came down hard on Jordan or pushed him in sports beyond what was safe for a developing boy, she didn't step in to defuse the intensity of his dad's expectations.

James was so seduced by Jordan's innate athletic talent that success on the field or in the gym was the only thing that mattered. He didn't just want to promote Jordan's glory. He wanted to share in it, and Jordan understood that without the all-encompassing excitement of sports, he had no value to his father.

Cory took his hand in hers, and her soft touch was more comfort than it probably should have been. Although she'd meant something to him when they'd grown close in Atlanta, at this point she was a virtual stranger. One with whom he shared a child, but a stranger nonetheless. How odd that she seemed to be able to read his mood and what he needed before the longing truly gelled inside his mind.

"How long has your book club been meeting?" Cory asked, effectively distracting his mother from thoughts about all the ways her older son was lacking.

"Over twenty years," his mom said with a smile. "Several of us have known each other since high school. We've been through a lot together. I'm lucky to have such amazing friends."

"That's wonderful." Cory nodded. "I always wanted to have lifelong friends." She gave a tight laugh. "Or any real girlfriends. I've never seemed to manage it."

"Are the women in Starlight not nice?" his mother asked, her gaze darting between Cory and Jordan. "I thought you said it's a close-knit community."

"It is," Jordan said, once again on the defensive. "Starlight is a great town."

His mother's feathery brows furrowed. "Then why—"

"It's probably my fault," Cory said quickly and slipped her hand from his. "I've been so busy with Ben that I haven't made much of an effort."

"You need to take care of yourself so you can take care of the baby," his mother advised, then pointed a finger at Jordan. "Are you not taking on enough of the childcare and household responsibilities?"

He felt his mouth drop open.

"Jordan is…um… It's not his fault." Cory glanced at him, her big eyes going even wider. "I need to take responsibility for my own happiness."

"Nonsense." Kathy rolled her eyes. "He's your partner and Ben's father. You know what they say— 'happy wife, happy life.'"

"I don't think Dad ever said that," Jordan said, then sighed when his mother's back went rigid. He'd told himself he wasn't going to bring up the past and his father's behavior. His mom had made her choice, and it was none of Jordan's business.

"You might be right," his mom said after a moment. "But he never prevented me from having friends."

Jordan threw up his hands. "I'm not stopping her from having friends."

"He's not," Cory added. "At all."

"You seem like a sweet girl," Kathy told Cory. "I imagine it's a bit awkward being a new mom but not a wife. Maybe after the two of you are married—"

"Mom, stop." Jordan stood and stalked to the fireplace, where the oak mantel still held framed photos of Jordan and Max as kids. "Cory can handle her own life, and no one is shunning her in Starlight because we're not married."

"Have you set a date?" his mom asked, undeterred. "Am I invited?"

Jordan felt his temples start to pound.

"What would you like Ben to call you?" Cory asked before Jordan could respond. "Grandma or Grammy or—"

"Mimi," his mother said, almost shyly. "I always thought my grandchildren would call me Mimi."

"Mom, that's—"

"Adorable," Cory interrupted. "I think that's so cute. Ben and his mimi are going to have so much fun together. I can already tell."

Jordan gave her an arch look he transformed into

a smile when he realized his mother was grinning broadly.

He couldn't remember ever seeing his mother smile like that. Just as he started to relax again, the back door opened and shut with a slam.

"Mom?"

"In the living room," Kathy called.

"Seriously?" Max's voice got louder as his footsteps sounded in the hallway. "Did someone else d—" His voice trailed off as he came to stand at the room's threshold, his hazel eyes taking in the scene. "Jordan. You're back."

"Why does everyone sound so shocked?" Jordan said. "I told you all I'd be here." He closed the distance between him and his younger brother in a few strides. His brother was taller now and had filled out from the gangly, bespectacled teen he'd been when Jordan left for college. Max had dark hair and their mother's gentle eyes. Her gentle spirit, as well. "You look good, Max. All grown-up."

"Five years will do that to a person," Max answered and returned Jordan's hug with a half-hearted embrace.

"You're welcome to visit Starlight anytime," Jordan said, ignoring the animosity in his brother's voice. "I have plenty of room."

"Some of us care about home," Max muttered, and Jordan hated the bitterness in his brother's gaze. He wished his relationship with his younger brother hadn't been a casualty of breaking away from his father's choke hold on his life, but there was little he could do to change that now.

"Come and meet your nephew," their mother said, as always trying to smooth over any friction that appeared between the brothers. Max had regularly been sick as a kid and stayed home with Kathy, while Jordan and his dad spent hours together through the football, wrestling and baseball seasons.

Max drew in a sharp breath. "You have a kid?"

Jordan wanted to explain the whole situation, to reveal his shock and worry over his suitability as a father. If anyone would understand, it was his brother.

"He has a fiancée, as well." Kathy stood and gestured to Cory. "Your brother must have forgotten his manners. Jordan, introduce your Cory to Max."

His Cory. Jordan scrubbed a hand over his jaw and tried not to think about how right it would feel if she were actually his.

"I'm Cory. It's nice to meet you," Cory said as she came to stand next to him, holding out a hand to his brother. "I'm sorry about the circumstances."

Max stared between the two of them and then glanced at Ben. "You two have a baby. But you aren't married?"

Jordan heard Cory's sharp intake of breath and shook his head. "Since when did you become the morality police?" he demanded of his brother.

"No disrespect." Instead of taking Cory's hand, Max stepped forward and gave her a hug. "Welcome to the nuthouse," he told Cory.

Wasn't that just the truth, Jordan thought. Honestly, he wouldn't blame Cory if she rented a car and headed back to Starlight and as far away from him as she could get.

"I'm glad to be here," she told his brother, although Jordan knew it must be a lie.

"We should check into the hotel," Jordan said as Max took Ben from their mother. The boy gazed up at his uncle for a long moment, then grinned. It embarrassed Jordan to no end that even his stuffy younger brother was more comfortable holding the baby than Jordan. What did that say about him? Nothing he wanted to admit.

"You aren't staying here?"

He couldn't make eye contact with his mother, not after the hurt in her voice.

"We'll see you tomorrow at the service," he said by way of an answer.

Max bounced Ben for a few more seconds before handing him to Cory. She gave both his brother and mom another hug. It felt as though she was as confused as Kathy about why they were checking into a hotel. To Jordan's eternal gratitude, she didn't question him.

In fact, she spoke very little on the short drive to downtown. That worked for him. There was nothing he could say that would adequately explain the riot of thoughts tumbling through his mind and heart.

Cory wasn't sure what she was thinking, knocking on the door separating her room from Jordan's later that afternoon. He'd made it clear he wanted to be alone. After the strange and surreal visit to his mother's house, she didn't blame him.

No one spoke directly about his father, although it was clear the man's presence continued to loom large for both Kathy and the two sons he'd left behind. Cory had never been so grateful for Ben, whose sweetness was about the only thing that made the time go by quickly.

She felt almost guilty she'd liked Jordan's mom. It was nice to have someone fussing over her son and talking about the baby like he was something more than a burden.

The good memories Cory had from spending time with her grandmother still meant the world to her, so of course she wanted that for her son. It definitely wouldn't come from her side of the family.

But she couldn't include Kathy in their lives without Jordan's approval. There had to be more to why he was so distant with his mom than simply time and the impact of Jordan living across the country. After all, he'd been in Starlight long enough to plan a visit to his hometown.

He opened the door after a few seconds, his hair

wild like he'd been pulling at the ends and his gaze shuttered.

"I talked to the lady at the front desk," she said with a bright smile. "She said there's a really good place to eat around the corner. It's not too cold, so Ben and I are going to walk over for an early dinner. Would you like to join us?"

He squinted at her like he was having trouble making sense of her words. Yes, she'd said them all on one rush of breath, but the invitation had been clear.

She pantomimed bringing a fork to her mouth. "Food. Eat. You and me."

"Why?"

Her turn to frown. "I'm hungry and figured you might be, as well."

"I was such a jerk earlier."

"At least you can admit it," she said with a laugh. "I get how hard it can be to go home, especially under the circumstances you're dealing with, but I'm not the enemy."

"I know." He ran a hand through his hair, and her stomach clenched as the muscles in his bicep flexed. She needed to get a grip on her awareness of this man. No point being distracted by his physical perfection when nothing could come of it. "In fact, I'm stellar at being my own worst enemy when it comes to being around my family."

Cory placed a hand on her stomach when a growl

escaped. "Grab a jacket and let's discuss your jerki-ness over dinner."

"Dinner is a yes. Talking about me being a jerk, hard pass." His voice was stern, but she could see his lips tugging up at the corners. And suddenly she desperately wanted to coax a smile from him.

They made their way to the nearby diner with Ben riding contentedly in his stroller. The air was chilled, so Cory had tucked a blanket around him and placed a wind barrier over the stroller's hood.

"Babies don't travel light," Jordan observed as Cory lifted Ben into her arms outside the restau-rant, and he folded the stroller to stow it near the front door.

"Not at all," she agreed with a laugh.

An older woman led them to a booth in the cor-ner and placed a high chair alongside it.

Cory sat the baby in it, supported from behind by his blanket. Ben looked around with his gaze wide, every experience and place new and fascinat-ing to him.

"I wish I could see the world through his eyes," Jordan said, echoing the thoughts in her head.

It both disturbed and delighted her that they were on the same wavelength. "I hope he never loses his curiosity," she said. "He's going to have the kind of unconditional love and support that makes him know he can do or try anything and still have a soft place to land with his mom."

"And his dad," Jordan said. "Although, I hope he doesn't try all the stupid stuff I did when I was younger."

The waitress appeared at the table and took their orders—a chicken club and side salad for Cory and a cheeseburger with sweet potato fries for Jordan.

She studied the man across the table for a long moment, then asked, "Were you a rebel back in the day? In Atlanta, you seemed like the mature one of the team, always guiding and mentoring the younger players."

"I learned some hard lessons that I didn't want to see other guys repeat." He glanced around the restaurant. "Most of my hell-raising was done in high school. Once I got out of Spokane, I lost the need to cause trouble."

"Because you didn't have to antagonize your father any longer?"

"I like to think I grew up, but I guess that had something to do with it." He shrugged, then turned his attention to Ben. "I was a master at pushing the old man's buttons." He wiggled a hand in front of the baby. Ben grabbed on to his father's finger, and Cory's breath caught in her throat at their two matching smiles. "I'm not planning to give this little guy a reason to cause trouble."

"Do boys need a reason?" Cory asked with a chuckle, which faded quickly at the look on Jordan's face. "You and your dad had a lot of problems."

"He was never satisfied with anything I did. No matter how much effort or energy I put into training, it wasn't enough. But at least if he was harping on me, that kept his focus off my mom. It's not going to be like that with Ben." He closed his eyes for a moment, like whatever he was thinking caused him pain. "I don't know how to be a dad, but I like to think I learned a lot about what not to do."

"That's a tough lesson."

When he looked at her again, he seemed miserable. "Would now be the appropriate time for you to point out how badly I messed up the reunion with my family today? I hadn't expected being back in that house to hit me the way it did. And then seeing my mom with Ben and how happy she seemed…"

"I'm glad she felt that way," Cory admitted, trying not to let too much emotion seep into her tone. "I know you aren't close with her, but maybe Ben can help change that. It's obvious she loves you."

He inclined his head. "Is it?"

"Yes. In fact—"

The waitress returned to the table at that moment with plates of food. Cory immediately regretted her choice of a salad instead of fries. The mountain of crispy sweet potatoes on Jordan's plate looked almost too good to resist.

"Go ahead." He handed her a ketchup bottle when they were alone again. "I remember that you're a food thief."

She wasn't sure what it meant that he remembered her habit of coveting food the people she was out to eat with ordered. They'd been at any number of team dinners together, but she couldn't remember ever "borrowing bites," as she liked to call it, from Jordan. Maybe she had without even thinking about it. She'd certainly tried to sit next to him when she could, because she always had more fun that way.

Her habit had bothered Kade to no end. By the end of their relationship, he seemed to relish pointing out that her inability to stick with the menu item she'd chosen said something about the inherent indecision built into her character.

She bit down on her cheek to hide her grin. "*Thief* is a harsh word." Her fingers brushed Jordan's when she took the ketchup from him, and awareness sparked across her skin. "I like options."

"The options from other people's plates," he countered.

"Sometimes."

Jordan pushed his plate closer. "Take a fry."

She tipped her chin and placed the condiment bottle on the table without opening it. "I'm happy with my salad."

"But you want a fry."

Her mouth watered as he popped one into his mouth. "So good. Crispy on the outside and fluffy inside, just like a good fry should be."

"Stop tempting me," she muttered.

"It's too much fun." He forked up a couple of fries and placed them next to her sandwich. "Now I'm going to have my feelings hurt if you don't eat one."

She wanted to say no, but they were too much to resist. The fry was indeed done to the perfect golden crispness, with the center remaining light and just the right amount of salt sprinkled on top.

"That a girl," Jordan coaxed with a smile, placing a few more on her plate. "It was worth giving in, right?"

Cory rolled her eyes. "I still have ten pounds of baby weight to lose. Salads are going to make that happen a lot quicker than fries."

"You look great."

"Sorry, I wasn't fishing for a compliment." She grabbed the ketchup and dumped a small pool onto her plate. If she was going to enjoy the fries, might as well add her favorite condiment into the mix.

"I know," Jordan told her, his deep voice once again sending her nerves into overdrive. "It's true, though. Motherhood agrees with you."

She tried not to read too much into his words, although she appreciated them. Being a mom wasn't the most glamorous, and with her grandmother sick on top of everything else, Cory had all but given up on self-care. "Thanks. You're going to get through your dad's service. I know it will be hard, but it's clear your mom is happy to have you here."

Jordan took a slow sip of the beer he'd ordered.

"I haven't been a very good son to her in the past few years."

"I saw the way she hugged you, Jordan. She's just waiting for an invitation back into your life."

"It's strange how I can hold on to my bitterness. She never once defended me when my dad was coming down hard or being an overbearing jerk. When I was twelve, I passed out in the middle of a wrestling tournament from dehydration and exhaustion. He got a doctor he knew to give me IV fluids, then put me in for the next match."

He set the bottle on the table and picked at the edge of the label with his thumbnail. "We were in town, so my mom happened to be there that day. She watched it happen and didn't say a word. She'd always bring me an ice cream sandwich later in my room. We wouldn't talk about whatever lecture I'd received or my aches and pains or the way he expected me to play through any injury without complaint. We'd just sit together in the glow of my nightstand light and eat our ice cream. That's when I felt the closest to her, although now I hate ice cream."

"No one hates ice cream," Cory argued gently.

"With the passion of a thousand burning suns." Jordan chuckled. "His behavior wasn't her fault, but I couldn't untangle her from him."

"Now you have a chance. With your brother, as well."

"I barely know my brother. My dad and I spent

so much time away from the house at games and tournaments and sports camps, it felt like we were two different families living under the same roof."

"Do you want that to change?"

He was quiet for several seconds before he nodded. "Yes."

"Then you'll make it happen"

"You make it sound easy."

She shook her head. "I gave up on easy a while ago. But worth it is a different story." Cory wanted to help him mend the tattered fabric of his bond with his mother. Both for Jordan's sake and for their son's.

Chapter Six

The late-winter sun lit a burnished sky the next day as Jordan's father was buried. It was still hard to believe the old man was gone, and Jordan couldn't quite shake the feeling of his shadow looming over the ones he'd left behind.

But Jordan had taken Cory's words to heart and made an effort with both his mom and his brother. He half expected them to rebuff his attempts to make peace. In this case, the prodigal son returning didn't feel worthy of any type of welcome home.

Instead, they'd shifted to assimilate him without question, as if everything that had come before was simply water under the bridge. He couldn't imagine it would be that easy to find balance and function better than they had before. But he was so damn grateful to think he might have a chance that he didn't examine or question their acceptance too closely.

With Cory at his side, he'd even managed to endure a number of awkward conversations with people who knew him as a kid, many of whom wanted to talk about his days in the NFL. Jordan was shocked how many of them had followed his career with avid interest, and he was reminded again of how much he appeared to have given up when he retired.

For him, he'd walked away without a second thought, the love of the game waning so much that staying wasn't worth it. Not with egocentric, fame-hungry guys like Kade becoming the ones who appeared to be the future of the league. Men who were more interested in being featured in highlight reel videos on the various sports channels each week or the size of a sponsorship payout their agents could negotiate as opposed to playing the game they were supposed to love.

Jordan's father had urged him to do more advertising and schmoozing with company execs and less enjoying his life on and off the field, only solidifying Jordan's understanding that he wasn't a match for the sport any longer.

Since leaving football, he'd gotten into an easy routine of working at the bar and taking advantage of the outdoor recreational activities around Starlight, but Cory and Ben had already changed his focus. If one thing had become clear during this trip, it was that he wanted them in his life. How that would look and whether she'd agree to it were a different matter entirely.

He exhaled a long breath as his mother wrapped him in a tight hug after walking them to the car. It amazed him how well she seemed to be coping with his dad's death. There were still a few women in the house, friends from book club who'd stayed to help her clean up after the reception that followed the funeral service.

Jordan was glad she wasn't alone.

"I'll call you in a couple of days," he said, pulling back. "If you need anything—"

"Having you here is what I needed." She patted his cheek, then glanced at Cory, who'd just strapped Ben into his car seat. "And meeting my grandson. You both have given me a reason to smile again."

"I'm glad, Mom."

"Now we just need to plan a wedding."

Jordan heard Cory's sharp intake of breath and resisted the urge to cringe. He might appreciate the progress he'd made in repairing his relationship with his mother, but he couldn't deny that the gains were built on a lie. He and Cory weren't together, and she'd given no indication she wanted a relationship with him.

If he had to guess, he'd say that if not for the

promise she'd made to her grandmother, she might not have even told him about his son.

He swallowed back the anger that clogged his throat at the thought. He'd missed the first six months of Ben's life and supporting his son through the trauma of his heart surgery, but Jordan was determined not to miss anything more.

"We're taking our time," he said, not exactly an outright lie. The more of those he could avoid, the better.

"Well, I've learned time is precious," his mother said with a glance at the back seat of the car, where Ben was chewing on his fist. "I'm not losing any more of it. In fact, I've made a decision."

"Okay." Jordan hoped his smile was encouraging as opposed to apprehensive.

"I'm coming to Starlight."

Cory made a choking sound next to him, and he purposely widened his smile. "I'd love that, Mom. Let me check the calendar when I get back home—"

"I'll be there on Friday," his mother told him with a nod. "I've already arranged for Marylou to water my plants."

Jordan swallowed. "How long are you planning to stay?"

"At least a week. Maybe longer." His mother reached out a hand and squeezed his arm. "I hope it's okay. I want to spend time with you and my grandson." She glanced around Jordan to smile at Cory. "And my future daughter-in-law."

"I mean…" Jordan searched his mind for an appropriate response. One that didn't involve him hurting his mom's feelings. That was the last thing he wanted. Well, maybe not the last. The last thing he wanted was his mother in Starlight for an extended stay.

He could see her eyes begin to dim as he tried and failed to formulate his words. She'd just buried her husband of over three decades. Jordan couldn't reject her outright, no matter the trouble he was about to get himself into.

"We'd love to have you stay with us." He pulled Cory closer to him, ignoring her squeak of protest. "Right, honey?"

"Of course," she murmured, and he was impressed her voice didn't waver. "We'd love to show you around town, and it would be wonderful for Ben to spend more time with his mimi."

Kathy's face brightened. "I can babysit while you two have date nights. I know it's hard to find time for romance with a little one around."

"Romance," Cory repeated, sounding not quite as sure as she had a few moments earlier.

"I promise I won't be an imposition," his mom said, then looked over her shoulder. "I should let you all start the drive. The timing is a bit strange, but the book-club ladies and I are having a meeting. They're such a comfort to me."

"What book are you reading?" Cory asked, apropos of nothing.

Jordan stared at her. How could she think about anything other than the fact that his mom was coming to town?

"Oh, it's an amazing personal development book." Kathy's gaze darted to Jordan, and she gave a sheepish smile. "Mainly geared toward women. It's called *Me First*. The ladies chose it because they figured I needed to learn how to make myself a priority after your father's death. I spent too much time giving away my power to him."

And the hits just kept on coming. Jordan had never thought of his mother other than as a helpmate to his dad. He would never have guessed that she possessed the self-realization to want to change and grow. Had that always been a part of her, a piece he'd overlooked because of his own anger?

Cory nodded as if everything coming out of his mom's mouth made complete sense. Impossible when his world was spinning out of control. "I'll have to check that out."

"Yes." Kathy reached out and squeezed Cory's hand. "We can have our own mini book club while I'm in Starlight."

"I'd like that."

"We need to go," Jordan said, unable to stand in

the front yard of his childhood home and feign things being normal for one more moment.

After another round of hugs from his mom, they got in the car and started toward the highway that led out of town.

He could feel Cory's assessing gaze on him but kept his eyes firmly on the road. There was no way he could mask the emotions swirling through him, and he wasn't ready to share them.

"What are we going to do?" she asked after checking on Ben in the back seat.

A quick glance in the rearview mirror showed the baby happily gumming the plastic ring of keys Cory had given him when she put him in the car.

"Apparently," Jordan grumbled, "you and my mom are going to start your own book club."

Out of the corner of his eye, he saw Cory stiffen. "It sounds like a good book."

"My mother didn't do one ounce of self-reflection during my childhood. So now I'm supposed to believe she's suddenly ready to be enlightened by some pop psychology tome?"

"I think it's nice she's trying to grow and change." Hearing Cory stand up for his mom both annoyed him and made him feel petty because of his irritation. "People can change, you know."

"Well, it's the opposite of nice that she's coming to Starlight and expecting to stay with us." He flicked a glance in Cory's direction. "You understand, right?"

"Of course," she answered tightly. "There is no us."

"So what are we supposed to do?" He shook his head. "What am I supposed to do? My mom wants to get to know a baby that I've just met. She wants to form a relationship with a fiancée that I don't have."

"Those are valid points." Cory turned to him. "We'll figure it out. It's figure-outable, just like my grandma always said."

Jordan blew out a long breath. "I sure hope your grandma knew what she was talking about."

Cory stood outside the coffee shop where she and Jordan were scheduled to meet the following day, nerves fluttering through her stomach like a renegade gang of spastic butterflies. After last night at the hotel, she was out of money and options.

They'd spent most of the drive home from Spokane working out how to manage his mom's visit. In the end, they'd come up with a plan to continue acting like they were a couple. Cory would be introduced in town as his long-distance girlfriend turned fiancée, and she'd stay in that role until his mom left town. She'd spent one final night in the hotel but would move into his house later that afternoon.

In fact, Jordan had suggested they plan their fake engagement to last for a full month. After that, they could break up but remain friends, or at least tell that story to the close-knit community of Starlight. She'd considered Jordan a friend at one point and wanted him to be more. But she had the feeling he didn't trust her or her motives at this point. Not that she blamed him. Wives and girlfriends of professional athletes sometimes got a bad rap because of the behavior of a select few. Most of the women Cory had met from the team were nice, although some of them got a little too caught up in the lifestyle.

She told herself that it didn't matter what he thought of her. Ben was the priority, and this temporary farce would ensure her son spent plenty of time with his father. It was a bonus that Ben would get to know his grandma, as well.

Cory had gotten used to putting the needs of her son above her own. Every time she thought of those first few days in the hospital and the terror of being told he'd need heart surgery, she knew that she could make it through anything as long as her child remained healthy and happy.

So what if her body seemed to be strangely aware of Jordan? Every move he made caught her attention in a way she didn't want or appreciate. It was going to feel like torture to pretend to be close to him but keep her emotions—and even more so her desire— out of the equation.

But she'd do it for Ben. Anything for her baby.

She balanced him on one hip as she entered Main Street Perk, amazed by the crowd of people filling the café tables in the middle of the afternoon. Clearly the coffee shop was a popular part of Starlight's downtown business scene. Ben looked around with wide eyes, and she smoothed a hand over the back of his head to ground herself before heading toward the table where Jordan sat near the front of the shop.

"Hey, babe," he said as she approached, his voice carrying across the room.

Cory felt color rise to her cheeks as the two baristas behind the counter openly stared at her. Oh yes. The women of Starlight were well aware of Jordan. She'd always hated the attention she received as Kade's girlfriend and the way other women would eye her up and down like they were trying to assess how easy it would be to poach her man.

She reminded herself Jordan didn't belong to her, even as she reached out to hug him when he stood. To her utter shock, he dropped a lingering kiss on her mouth, a public claiming, so to speak.

The butterflies took flight again, and Cory did her best to smother them. This was all an act, she told herself. They had only a few days to make their relationship believable to the people of this town before his mom arrived.

No time for subtlety.

Ben cooed and reached for his father, making Cory's breath catch. "Come to Daddy," Jordan said, a little too loudly.

Cory laughed. "Maybe find a different way to say that next time."

The blush that rose on Jordan's cheeks loosened

some of her nerves, but she realized he was truly disconcerted. He glanced around to make sure no one could overhear him. "I don't know what the hell I'm doing being a dad."

"You've got it." She transferred Ben to his arms. "It would be more believable if you didn't look like you were going to throw up."

Jordan's jaw tightened. "I'll get used to it."

"It's not like a toothache." She took the seat across from him. "I promise you'll be a natural before you know it."

Two cups of coffee and a plate of muffins sat on the checked tablecloth.

"I got you a sugar-free latte," he told her as he sat down again. "Although, I guess I don't know if that's still what you drink."

"It's great," she whispered, blown away he remembered her favorite coffee drink from the time they'd spent together in Atlanta. Seriously, how was she going to walk away from this man in a month?

A woman approached the table, curiosity obvious on her pretty features. She was tall and lithe, her chocolate-colored hair pulled into a loose bun. To Cory, she looked more like a high-end professional than a woman who belonged in a small-town coffee joint. "Hey, Jordan."

"Hi, Mara," he said calmly, like he showed up in the coffee shop every day with a strange woman and baby. "Nice muffins today."

"Thanks. I appreciate a guy who appreciates my muffins." She flashed a saucy grin before her gaze turned serious. "Parker said he stopped by Trophy Room last night for a drink with Nick and Finn. Tanya mentioned you were out of town for your dad's funeral. We're all sorry for your loss."

Cory watched Jordan's reaction closely. He started to go tense, but Ben patted a chubby hand on the tip of his nose. One side of Jordan's full mouth pulled into a smile, and relief coursed through Cory.

"I appreciate that," he answered, then gestured to Cory. "Have you met my fiancée? This is Cory Hall."

Cory choked on the swallow of coffee she'd just taken as the other woman's mouth dropped open.

"I don't believe I have," Mara said, eyebrows lifting almost to her hairline.

The grin he bestowed on Cory was filled with tenderness. "Sweetheart, this is Mara Johnson. She runs the coffee shop and is Starlight's master baker."

"I've heard a lot about you," Cory lied, because that was the plan. Jordan had told her most people in Starlight came through the coffee shop at some point during the week, so it made sense to have their first date there.

"Interesting." Mara glanced between Cory and Jordan. "I've heard nothing about you, but I'll admit I'm quite curious. Apparently, our friendly neighborhood bar owner has been keeping his private life very private."

"I can't wait to get to know all of Jordan's friends." Panic made Cory's chest tighten. She didn't like to lie, so she had spent a lot of time working out how to explain her sudden appearance without outright falsifying information. "You can blame me for the secrecy." She licked her suddenly dry lips. "Ben had some health issues when he was born, so I needed to stay in Michigan until the doctors cleared him for travel."

Mara made a soft tsking sound and touched Ben's arm. "Oh, sweet boy. You look perfect."

"He is perfect," Jordan said, and Cory blinked away tears.

"He had heart surgery five days after he was born to repair a narrowed aortic valve."

"Jordan." Mara's hazel eyes widened. "Why didn't you tell us anything? People would have happily pitched in at the bar to take care of things so you could go back. How old is Ben now?"

"Six months," Cory offered before Jordan could speak. His eyes had gone dark, and she could imagine what he was thinking. How angry he must feel that he wasn't told about the baby, so he missed the chance to be with them during the trauma of surgery and recovery.

"Jordan flew back to Michigan whenever his schedule allowed. I really wanted to keep everything private." She gave the other woman a watery smile she didn't have to manufacture. Just talking about that time made her emotional. "To be honest, Jordan and I have been through some ups and downs. We needed to get to a solid place before…" She drew in a deep breath. "We needed to be solid."

"And now we are." He covered her hand with his big one, the callus on his palm tickling her skin, and then looked at Mara. "I'm hoping you, Brynn and Kaitlin will help her get her bearings in Starlight."

"And a job," Cory added.

"You have a job," Jordan countered, thick brows furrowing. "It's called being a mom."

"I can be a great mom and also work if that's what I choose." Cory spoke slowly, like she was talking to a toddler. Of course, they hadn't discussed her working yet. The list of things they needed to go over seemed never ending.

Before Jordan had a chance to respond, Mara chuckled. "That's exactly right. Brynn is balancing work and motherhood, and she has little Remi plus a ten-year-old. I managed it most of my daughter's life. Don't worry, Cory. We'll help you figure it out." She pulled a cell phone out of the back pocket of the jeans she wore. "Although, I'm not babysitting. Babies aren't my thing."

Jordan frowned. "You have a six-year-old. Evie was once a baby."

"I barely made it out alive," Mara said with a mock shudder before winking. "Just kidding. I love my daughter, and she was adorable. Your little guy is adorable, too. I can admire him from afar." She handed her phone to Cory. "Go ahead and put your number into my contacts. I'll arrange a time for all of us to get together. I'm sure Tanya has made you feel welcome already."

Cory darted a questioning glance at Jordan.

"She hasn't met everyone at the bar yet," he said, almost apologetically. "Tanya's going to give me a ration of grief for not telling her about this."

Mara laughed again. "Good luck with that." She turned her attention to the counter when one of the baristas called her name. "It was nice to meet you, Cory. Welcome to Starlight."

"Thanks," Cory said quietly, then stared at the half-eaten pastry on her plate as the other woman walked away. Her mouth felt like it was filled with sawdust, and her stomach cramped from anxiety.

"I don't know if I can do this," she told him. "It's too much. If she's an example of the type of people who live in this town, I don't want to lie to them."

Jordan scrubbed a hand over his jaw, then closed his eyes when Ben rested his head on his shoulder. "It's for Ben. We're doing this for our son. You'll move into my house today, right? Are you comfortable with that?"

Cory blew out a long breath. Hadn't she just reminded herself that she would do anything for Ben? "Okay, yes," she whispered. "But just know I hate every part of it."

Jordan nodded and averted his gaze. "Duly noted," he said through clenched teeth.

It was going to be a long few weeks pretending this was her life and not desperately wishing it to be real.

Chapter Seven

Jordan did a double take when Cory walked into the bar later that night. She wasn't carrying the baby and looked as beautiful as he'd ever seen her. Her dark hair had been curled at the ends, and she wore a pair of fitted jeans that hugged her curves, along with a red sweater in a material so soft he wanted to reach out and touch it. He wanted to touch her, and the knowledge their pretend relationship gave him the freedom to do just that made it hard to concentrate on anything but his desire.

They'd agreed that he would mention her and Ben to his employees before formally introducing them so that he could answer questions and get everyone used to the idea of the boss having a secret family before they met.

He'd talked to Tanya, Madison and the rest of the crew earlier that afternoon during an impromptu staff meeting. The announcement that Jordan had a fiancée and a baby had been met with a range of reactions—from straight-up shock to gentle teasing to hearty congratulations. Tanya had grilled him on the situation while Madison stared with amused astonishment. True to her form, his prickly, if talented, head chef seemed to enjoy watching him squirm under a barrage of pointed questions.

But he'd gotten through it, and although Tanya sent him admonishing looks as she served drinks to the regulars, he knew she'd make sure the rest of the staff fell in line to support Cory and make sure there were no rumors spread about her.

Jordan didn't quite understand his protective streak when it came to Cory. He still held plenty of resentment about her keeping his son from him. He wasn't sure if he could truly trust her, despite his attraction. The attraction part had him swallowing back a growl as several male heads turned to check her out as she approached the bar.

He hadn't been kidding when he said motherhood agreed with her. To his deep consternation, Jordan wasn't the only one who seemed to notice.

He ran a tight ship at Trophy Room. The bar might look like a throwback to a small-town tavern with its paneled walls and scuffed wood bar, but he wanted everyone who walked in the door to feel comfortable. He didn't tolerate rude and offensive comments from customers or rowdy crowds, although he couldn't exactly stop his patrons from admiring a pretty woman.

Certainly he couldn't give in to the urge to knock some heads together until they stopped looking at his fiancée.

His fake fiancée, he reminded himself.

"Hey, ba—" He cleared his throat, then lifted a hand to wave. Cory had told him in no uncertain terms she would not answer to the term *babe*, which made him smile and also tempted him to call her that all the more just to elicit a reaction.

Her mouth quirked at the corner like she was trying to hide a smile. "Hi, hon," she said, smooth as his favorite single-malt scotch. She placed her hands on the bar, elegant fingers spread over the burnished wood, and leaned forward.

Like a moth drawn to a flame, he bent his head, heart hammering when she pressed her soft mouth to his.

He barely registered the gasps that came from the patrons around him and had to resist the urge to lift her over the bar and into his arms, caveman style.

"This is a surprise," he told her when she pulled back.

Her thin shoulders lifted and lowered. "Mara put me in touch with her friend Brynn, who recommended a babysitter." She bit down on her lower lip and then offered him a smile. "I missed you, so once I got Ben down for the night, I thought I'd stop in for a visit."

Blood roared through Jordan's brain. He knew she was playing a part right now, but the look in her eye made him believe every word. It was hard as hell not to want her to be speaking the truth.

"Are you going to introduce us?" a feminine voice asked behind him. "Or just stand there making googly eyes all night?"

He turned to see Tanya and Madison staring at him with twin smirks on their faces. Of all the times for his chef to make an appearance at the front of the house, it would have to be this moment.

"I vote for googly eyes," Ray Monning said from his bar stool. The older man winked at Cory. "I mean that in the most respectful way, ma'am."

"Understood," she said with a wide grin and held out a hand. "I'm Cory, Jordan's fiancée." She hitched a thumb in Jordan's direction. "Googly eyes aren't usually my thing, but I make an exception for this guy."

Jordan's heart melted just a little bit as Ray shook her hand with wide-eyed astonishment. He was one of the regulars, but his history in town was spotty at best. He had trouble holding down a job and stuck mostly to himself since his wife had left him several years earlier. Jordan rarely had to refuse to serve customers, but he would if someone got out of hand.

Ray never got out of hand, but most people in town overlooked him. He was just an old-timer who'd fallen through the cracks when it came to living a life society deemed successful. He wore the same ratty flannel every day and was often in need of a shower. Jordan mostly felt sorry for him and did what he could to be a sympathetic shoulder, but Ray wasn't much for conversation.

Now he was looking at Cory like she was the sun shining down on him. Jordan certainly understood the feeling.

"I didn't know the barman had a fiancée," Ray said, drawing out the syllables of that last word as he glanced between Cory and Jordan.

"He kept the secret from all of us," Madison added. "Sneaky schmuck."

To her credit, Cory didn't flinch at the other woman's snarky tone. If anything, her smile grew brighter. "I'm here now, and I'm looking forward to getting to know everyone." Her gaze zeroed in on Madison. "I hear that your food is amazing. Fries are my favorite, so I can't wait to try yours. It probably sounds strange, but I'm a little bit of a connoisseur. A perfect French fry is difficult to master."

Jordan flinched as his chef narrowed her eyes. She tended to be just shy of outright confrontational when anyone even hinted at judging her culinary skills. "Well, then. It's my dearest hope I can live up to your high standards."

"Be nice," Tanya whispered under her breath.

Cory only continued to smile, not offering an antagonizing reply but not backing down, either. Add backbone to the list of things that Jordan found attractive about her. The list was getting longer by the second.

A couple gestured to Jordan from the far end of the bar. It was easy to get distracted by Cory, as well, but he needed to keep his wits about him.

"I'll be right back," he said, tossing a towel over his shoulder.

"Come to the kitchen with me," Madison ordered Cory, crooking her finger. "I'm working on a new dipping sauce for the manchego cheese croquettes. I need a discerning palate to taste test for me."

"Unnecessary," Jordan said as he moved past, throwing a beseeching glance toward Tanya. "Help," he mouthed.

She shrugged in return. "You should have mentioned her earlier."

The wife of the couple waved to him again. Thirsty patrons he couldn't ignore. He gave one last glance over his shoulder. "You can wait for me," he called to Cory.

"I don't bite," Madison said.

Cory nodded and stepped forward. "I appreciate that. Lead on. You had me hooked at the word *cheese*."

Worlds colliding, Jordan thought, his heart still

beating at a rapid pace as Cory followed Madison into the kitchen and out of his sight. He hadn't expected his worlds to collide so soon.

Anxiety pounded through him like a fierce thunderstorm. Maybe he needed to serve himself a drink along with his customers. Tanya gave him a funny look, and he forced a steadying breath and pasted a smile on his face. As if he didn't have enough dealing with the shock of being a father, he'd never imagined how stressful it would be to have a fake fiancée.

Cory was used to being underestimated.

Her mom had done it for most of Cory's life and then she'd spent her relationship with Kade being either coddled or condescended to, so she didn't misinterpret the willowy chef's invitation to her kitchen as anything but the gauntlet it was.

If she had any question, Jordan's terrified glance had confirmed her suspicions. Even Tanya, the spirited bartender, had squeezed Cory's arm as she walked past. "Good luck," the other woman murmured. "Just don't cry. Tears are like blood in the water when the sharks are circling for Madison."

A dire warning for sure.

"Sit," Madison ordered when they entered the bar's kitchen. The woman flicked her wrist at the line cook currently chopping vegetables on an oversize butcher block. "Out," she told him.

He swallowed and nodded, then dropped his knife and practically raced out of the room.

"Is everyone around here afraid of you?" Cory asked conversationally as she took a seat on the metal stool positioned in front of the stainless-steel counter. Despite all of her bluster, Cory liked Madison. As far as she could tell, they had very little in common, but somehow the prickly woman felt like a kindred spirit.

"Fear and respect go hand in hand in my kitchen," Madison said simply.

"They aren't mutually exclusive, you know."

The other woman shot her a glare. "Big words. Are you some kind of fancy scholar?"

That made Cory laugh out loud. "Hardly. Are you a classically trained chef?"

Madison's mouth thinned. "As a matter of fact, yes."

"What do you like most about cooking?"

"No one has ever asked me that. I like your earrings. They're unique."

Cory touched a finger to one of the thin gold hoops with multicolored stones strung through them. Pride snaked along her spine. "Thank you. I made them. But you're avoiding my question, and it's a fair one for someone who makes her living in the kitchen. I read the online reviews of the bar and the food you serve. People rave about it."

"I'm good."

"I'd say you're more than good. When you have

that much positive feedback for doing work that's so personal, it must be because you have a true passion for it. I'm curious what that is."

"You know this is supposed to be an interrogation of you." Madison crossed her arms over her chest. Her white chef's coat and black pants were basically shapeless, but it was clear she had an enviable figure, all long legs and slim curves. It didn't look as though she was wearing makeup, which in no way detracted from her creamy skin and rosy mouth. A mouth that was pressed into an unforgiving line, something Cory could almost appreciate. She had a feeling this woman wouldn't take grief from anyone.

"You're interrogating me?" Cory inclined her head. "I wouldn't have guessed. I thought I was just here to eat."

"Jordan gave us a convoluted story about your long-distance relationship. He wasn't convincing."

Cory drew in a breath. "It's complicated."

"That I believe." Madison took a trio of perfectly round cheese balls out of the fryer and plated them. She poured two different kinds of sauces into matching ramekins, then placed them in front of Cory. "Tell me more."

"Oh, that smells divine." Cory dipped a piece of fried cheese into one of the creamy sauces and bit into it. The flavors exploded on her tongue, a kaleidoscope of savory and spice with just the hint of smoky sweetness. She closed her eyes so she could concentrate more fully on the bite. She didn't consider herself a foodie but could appreciate Madison's genius with flavors. "Is that paprika?"

"I have it shipped in from Hungary. The local grocery in Starlight doesn't carry anything worth buying as far as spices go."

"I didn't realize it made such a difference." Cory took another bite. "Wow. I could swim in a vat of that."

She glanced up as Madison let out a rusty laugh. "That would be disgusting."

"But worth it." Cory looked past the other woman. "Didn't I see that chicken satay skewers are the special tonight? My taste buds are advanced." She tried hard not to laugh as she said the words. Her idea of gourmet during her pregnancy had been fast-food chicken nuggets with a large fry and a strawberry milkshake. "I can definitely give you a worthwhile opinion on those, as well."

"You just told me you want to swim in garlic aioli. That's not exactly discriminating."

"You never told me why you like to cook," Cory said with a shrug.

"You never told me the real deal with you and Jordan."

Cory thought about how to handle this situation. She knew what Jordan would tell her. Lie. She needed to keep up the charade of them being a couple until his mother came and went. That was the agreement.

But she didn't want to lie. It had been hard enough when they were together in the coffee shop. Madison's gaze on her was far too knowing. Cory got the feeling the other woman would sniff out the deception, and Cory wouldn't get to be any sort of taste tester if she got on the chef's bad side.

"We have a baby together," she said because that was the truth.

"And you're engaged?"

"In a manner of speaking." Cory kept her focus on the plate. "Can I have a piece of chicken now?"

"Explain the manner of which you speak and I'll give you the best satay you've ever had."

"That's blackmail." Her mouth watered.

The other woman shrugged. "It will blow your mind." She glanced toward the kitchen door. "But I want the scoop before Jordan comes back here like some knight in shining flannel to rescue you."

"It's kind of wrong to look that good in flannel," Cory mused.

"Stop trying to change the subject."

"You're bossy," Cory said, pointing a finger. She felt oddly comfortable with the caustic chef.

"You're tougher than you look."

That compliment made a lightness infuse Cory's chest, but she didn't answer the question about Jordan. "I've heard you have trouble keeping your employees happy. Do you think that is a result of your bossy nature?"

"It's my kitchen," Madison reminded her.

"But you need people to want to be here with you. You can't do it alone."

"I hire good people and train them well."

"Are they loyal to you?"

"They respect my skill."

"Okay, Ms. Chef Miyagi." Cory made a face. "Wash on and wash off with your bad self. Who cares if people like you as long as they're afraid of you?"

"Do you want the chicken satay or not?"

"Of course I do. It smells amazing, and I'm hungry."

"Then tell me about the engagement."

Cory threw up her hands and then looked around the kitchen to make sure they were alone. She didn't need to tell this woman anything. They were strangers, and Madison worked for Jordan. That should tell Cory everything she needed to know about the other woman's loyalty.

Yet… Cory had no one in her life now that her grandmother was gone. Nobody in her corner. No friends. No support system of her own. She didn't think for a minute that she and Madison were destined to become besties and braid each other's hair or skip off to Vegas for a girls' weekend. There was something about the woman, however, that made

Cory believe she could be trusted. And Cory desperately wanted someone to know the truth. "It's fake, okay?" she blurted before she thought better of it. "Until I got to town this week, I hadn't seen Jordan since the one night we spent together."

"The night where you made the baby?"

"Yes, that night. Now please give me the satay."

"Okay, Ms. Sassy-Pants." Madison plated the food and placed it in front of Cory. "First, your strange little secret is safe with me. I'm trying to figure out why the two of you are bothering to make all of this up. Did Jordan know about the baby and he didn't want to be involved?"

Cory shook her head and cut off a sliver of chicken. "No. The complicated part was the truth. We were friends and then had one night together after I broke up with my long-term boyfriend. The next day Kade told the guys we were back together and getting engaged. He hadn't bothered to mention it to me, but Jordan believed him." Her chest ached at the memory, but she forced herself to breathe through it. She was leaving the past behind for the sake of her baby.

Instead she focused on Madison's food. As soon as the chicken hit her tongue, she moaned out loud. "This is obscene," she said after finishing the bite. "Does the Michelin-star guy know about you?"

"Small-town bars don't get Michelin stars," Madison said with a laugh.

"They should when the food is this spectacular." She pointed her fork at the chef. "You should get five stars."

"And that's not how the rating system works."

"Seriously, what are you doing here? You should have your own restaurant in some fancy upscale town or big city."

Madison's eyes went dark. "Been there, done that. The pressure didn't agree with me. Stop trying to change the subject. We were at the part where your boyfriend—"

"Ex-boyfriend," Cory corrected.

"Your ex-boyfriend," Madison amended. "When you call him Kade, does that mean Kade Barrington, the bad-boy darling of the NFL?"

"You makes him sound a lot more charming than he actually is."

"So what happened next?"

"Kade showed up at the hotel room I'd rented while I was looking for a place to stay. I tried to avoid him, but he eventually tracked me down. I'm pretty sure the girl at the reservation desk alerted him. He could be a real charmer when he wanted to."

"Sounds more like a real stalker," Madison observed.

Cory shrugged. She'd gotten so used to her ex-boyfriend's overbearing personality that it hadn't seemed odd at the time. But, yeah, Kade had crossed the line, and she'd let him. "I hadn't talked to Jordan since I left his place. Everything was too over-whelming, and I thought I had time to figure out my feelings. After Kade told me what he'd announced to the guys, I kicked him out of my room and went to find Jordan."

"Don't tell me he believed you'd gone back to that guy or used him for a night."

"He was gone," Cory murmured, placing her fork on the plate. As amazing as the food was, her stomach twisted into uncomfortable knots. "It was the postseason and there was already a question as to whether Jordan would return because of his injury. I don't know if the business with Kade had anything to do with it, or the timing simply worked out, but he left Atlanta and announced his retirement the following week."

"You didn't go after him?" Madison asked, curiosity clear in her tone.

"No." Embarrassment added to the uncomfortable feeling roiling in her gut. "I figured we were just together one night and he realized he didn't want anything to do with me. That's how it felt, anyway." She ran a hand through her hair, regretting the fact that she'd tried so hard to look nice tonight now that emotions from that time had risen to the surface. Jordan had walked away without even talking to her. That had been a clear indication of his feelings. There was a good chance she was imagining everything else—the connection and attraction that seemed to shimmer in the air between them.

"Then you realized you were pregnant," Madison added quietly when Cory didn't say anything else.

"I knew after the first ultrasound the baby wasn't Kade's." Cory pressed her lips together. "He tried to convince me to get back together with him anyway, but it wasn't going to work. I didn't want that life for my baby. The timing of the pregnancy…" She shook her head. "The baby was Jordan's. I know I should have tried harder to track him down, but I went back to Michigan and things just seemed to spiral out of control. My grandma was sick, so I moved in with her. I could barely process the thought of being a mom, let alone trying to negotiate it alongside a man I'd been with one time."

"That's a lot to deal with."

"I'm not proud of the choices I made, but I'm trying to make amends for them."

"Oh, honey." Madison chuckled. "Welcome to the club. We all have things we'd like a redo on. My list is a mile long."

Cory did her best to smile, although it felt a little wobbly at the edges. At the same time, she felt more at peace than she had in ages. She'd shared the truth of her circumstances with someone who didn't seem inclined to judge her for her mistakes. It felt like the first real step she'd taken toward the life she wanted to have. In fact, she wanted more of this feeling.

Madison was obviously wrestling with her own demons. What if they could be actual friends? What if Cory could put together her own tribe of women the way Jordan's mom had in her life? What if she made Starlight her home even after she and Jordan ended their pretend engagement?

"We should start a book club," she blurted, and Madison took a step back.

"Do I look like the joiner type?"

"You look like someone I want to hang out with."

"No one wants to hang out with me." Madison scoffed, but Cory saw color bloom on her cheeks. "Unless it's because I'm cooking for them."

"Then we'll start a cooking club," Cory said with a nod. "That's perfect."

"You're crazy."

"Crazy about me." Jordan's voice came from the door leading to the bar.

Madison looked at Cory, brow raised.

"Not a word of what I told you," Cory murmured. "We're friends. Friends don't snitch."

She thought the other woman might laugh in her face, but Madison only inclined her head. "Because snitches wind up in ditches," she said with a soft laugh.

"Not exactly my train of thought, but let's go with it." She climbed off her chair and turned to Jordan. "You're lucky to have someone with so much talent in your kitchen."

"Agreed," he said, then ran a hand through his hair as he glanced around. "By the way, Louis quit on his way out. He said he'd rather flip burgers at a fast-food dump than have you order him around."

"He's an idiot," the chef muttered.

"Also the fourth kitchen employee we've lost this month. We're going to run out of candidates in Starlight."

Madison's whole demeanor changed in an instant. "Then I'll do it all myself."

Jordan shook his head. "That won't work when we're busy on the weekends. You need help."

"I'm looking for work," Cory offered as she took a final bite of chicken. "Madison and I are going to start a cooking club, so the more I learn about the kitchen, the better. I can wait tables, too. I've done it before."

"No way." Jordan looked almost horrified. "I won't have my fiancée toiling away in the kitchen."

Cory felt her mouth drop open. "Um, what year is this? Did I miss the time traveling to Downton Abbey, where you're the lord of the manor and I'm the lowly servant wench?"

"Sounds like some kinky role-playing to me," Madison said, clearly enjoying Jordan's irritation.

"No, thanks," Cory told the chef, then turned fully to Jordan. "For your information, if I can work out childcare for Ben, I can apply for whatever job I want."

"It's my bar," he countered.

"It's my kitchen," Madison said. "Remember, our deal was I got full control of the food and my staff."

"You don't want to hire her." Jordan hitched a finger at Cory. "She has no experience, and she can barely boil water."

Cory narrowed her eyes, even though he was right. She regretted sharing funny stories with him about her long list of kitchen failures, never guessing that they would be thrown back in her face this way.

"You take two days off a week," Madison reminded Jordan. "I'll arrange her shifts so she works those nights as well as the weekend." Her crystalline blue gaze switched to Cory. "That way you'll have less childcare scheduling to manage."

"That sounds great." Cory couldn't hide her smile.

"*That* sounds like the worst idea in the history of ideas," Jordan said, sounding exasperated.

Madison gave a thumbs-up to Cory and ignored Jordan. She grabbed a small pad of paper and a pen from a nearby counter, scribbled something on it and handed the paper to Cory. "Here's my number. Think about the logistics. Discuss it with your fiancé if you need to."

"Doubtful," Cory muttered.

"Call me tomorrow if you want to talk more about what I'd expect. I don't go easy on the people who work for me."

"I'm not looking for easy," Cory said. "We can make plans for the club idea, too."

"This is not happening," Jordan said, arms akimbo.

"I'm heading back home." Cory turned and planted a smacking kiss on Jordan's cheek. "We'll talk later, hon. Nice to meet you, Chef."

Madison chuckled. "It's been interesting."

Ignoring Jordan's heavy scowl, Cory walked away, looking forward to this new challenge.

Chapter Eight

"I'll help you find a different job," Jordan said a few days later as he watched Cory making a list of instructions in her neat penmanship. "One that will make you happy."

She didn't look up from her writing as she answered, "I think working with Madison will make me happy."

"Said no one ever. I don't know a single person who would say Madison Maurer makes them happy, other than through her food."

"Her mom might argue with you. Most mothers are made happy by their children." Cory straightened, her brows furrowed. "Except maybe mine, but most others. At least that's what I want to believe."

He felt his mouth open and close in stunned shock at her eternal optimism. Other than when she was giving him grief, Cory always tried to look at the bright side of a situation. It made him feel like a regular Eeyore in comparison. "That's an argument for another time. Once we finish this one."

"We aren't arguing, and there's no need for discussion." She glanced at her watch. "I need to leave in fifteen minutes. Don't want to be late for my first day on the job."

He closed his eyes for a moment, trying to figure out if it was worth making one last-ditch effort to change her mind. He'd been trying all day. Cory had been asleep when he got home last night, or at least her door remained closed. The door of the room across the hall from hers had been cracked. He'd crept in to watch Ben sleeping in the soft glow of the night-light plugged in next to the makeshift changing table.

Jordan's heart had tightened almost painfully as his son's chest rose and fell with steady breaths. The boy wore fire-truck pajamas, and his arms and legs were spread out in a great imitation of a starfish. Jordan tended to sleep the same way even as an adult, and he wondered if something like that could be passed down. It still amazed him that he'd helped create this beautiful baby.

Of course, Cory had done the heavy lifting so far, which was often the way with mothers, in his experience. But he'd become part of the equation, even though he wasn't yet comfortable with his abilities.

"It's probably too soon," he told Cory, taking a different tack. "Ben needs to be more settled here before you start work. What if he needs something?"

She inclined her head as she studied him like she couldn't understand a word coming out of his mouth. "Even way out in the woods, you're only fifteen minutes from town. If there's an emergency, call me."

Before he could answer, the baby monitor on the counter crackled, and he heard the sounds of Ben's quiet fussing. The boy had such an easygoing temperament but always woke with a few minutes of postnap crankiness. Another thing he could have inherited from Jordan.

Cory held up the paper with the instructions she'd been writing. "I have a list for you here with his feeding schedule and other pertinent details, but let's start with the first lesson." She winked at him. "Diaper changing."

Jordan shook his head slowly. "I've never changed a diaper."

"I figured as much by the way you conveniently disappear any time he needs to be changed."

"It's not convenient. It's purposeful."

She laughed as she walked past him and squeezed his arm. "Get ready to become an expert."

Jordan had never considered becoming an expert on diapers, or anything to do with fatherhood, but he dutifully followed Cory. She was right. He did tend to pick and choose the parenting duties he was comfortable performing.

Mostly he liked being in the role of entertainer, making both Ben and Cory smile with his funny faces or games of peekaboo. Although Cory told him Ben was big for his age, the baby still seemed so breakable to Jordan, especially after what he'd been through.

As soon as they walked into the bedroom, Cory began to talk to Ben, telling him in her soothing voice that he'd be spending the afternoon and evening with Daddy and she knew they'd have lots of fun.

Jordan found her words oddly reassuring, as if hearing her say them out loud made him able to believe they were true.

She stopped in front of the crib that Jordan had borrowed and put together. He needed to do more to make this room welcoming. Before Ben, it had been an overflow storage room, and it certainly didn't look like a nursery. No doubt Jordan's mom would notice that immediately.

"So you have to pick him up to change the diaper," Cory explained in a patient voice.

"He likes you to get him up from a nap," Jordan argued. "That's what he's used to."

"He'll get used to his daddy."

Jordan felt like the biggest fool. How hard was it

to be a father? He had plenty of friends who raised kids, both in Starlight and back when he was in the NFL. Huge, hulking bruisers on the field who'd cradle their babies in their arms, mostly like a football, in Jordan's opinion. But they'd done it.

What the hell was wrong with him?

He swallowed back his irrational fear and leaned over the crib. "Don't cry," he commanded, earning a chuckle from Cory.

Ben shoved his fist in his mouth and stared as Jordan lifted the baby into his arms. "Okay, that was easy enough." He made a face as a rancid scent rose in the air. "Oh no. I think something crawled into the crib with him and died."

"He probably woke up because he pooped." Cory smoothed a hand over the boy's head. "Did Mommy's big man make a big poopy?"

"I hope Mommy's not going to make Daddy run the poopy gauntlet his first time out of the gate," Jordan said, matching her singsong tone.

"One hundred percent you are changing this diaper. Don't be a wimp."

He raised a brow. "I have never been accused of being wimpy."

"I think I just made the accusation."

"Fine." He gripped the baby's torso and held him at arm's length. "Let's do this doo-doo duty."

"So clever," Cory murmured with a soft laugh.

Jordan shouldn't like making her laugh as much

as he did. Or take so much pleasure in the way she smiled at him. She smiled a lot. He needed to keep reminding himself that he wasn't special. Not to her.

He placed Ben on the changing pad Cory had brought with her, which sat on top of the pine dresser in the baby's room. The boy kicked up his feet like he wanted to give Jordan easy access to his dirty bottom.

"I believe in you," Cory said, placing a hand on Jordan's lower back. The words were said in a teasing manner, but they meant something. Like her laugh, the vote of confidence made him feel like he could do anything.

He unbuttoned Ben's one-piece romper but frowned as he pulled the baby's legs out of the soft fabric, exposing his chest. "He doesn't have a scar." Jordan glanced at Cory. "If he had heart surgery…"

"They went in through his back," she explained, her tone tight. "After you finish the diaper, you can undress him and see it."

"I wasn't doubting you," Jordan quickly told her. "It just surprised me."

"I understand."

But it didn't sound like she understood. "Grab a few wipes," she told him and proceeded to walk him through changing a dirty diaper while Jordan did his best not to gag or make faces at the mess and the smell.

"How does a kid that small produce so much

poop?" he asked as he placed the final wet wipe into the bag Cory had given him.

"You should have seen the blowouts he used to have when he was really young. At least the poop is somewhat contained now."

Jordan cringed, then picked up a clean diaper as Ben continued to wriggle on the table. He seemed in a much better mood now that the mess had been taken care of, and Jordan couldn't blame him.

As he started to place the diaper under the baby, Cory moved forward and turned it around. "Tabs go from back to front," she told him, but he was struggling to focus because she was so close that she was pressed against his side. Awareness zipped through him. They might have only spent one night together, but his body remembered hers.

Damn, he needed to get out more. There was absolutely nothing sexy about changing his baby's diaper, but he couldn't seem to stop his reaction. He wanted to be closer to her. He wanted more—more than he knew was right based on their arrangement, and he'd guess far more than she was willing to give.

As they made it through the diaper-changing lesson, Cory patted Jordan's arm. "Nice work for a newbie," she said, not meeting his gaze. "I'll take him while you wash your hands." Had she sensed his awareness of her or noticed the unexpected intimacy of the moment the way he did?

While he finished washing, she took Ben into

the family room, where he sat on a blanket playing with a toy piano in front of him. She'd taken off the baby's romper, and Jordan sucked in a breath as he noticed the one-inch scar from an incision that ran next to the boy's spine. "I can't believe what he went through." He dropped down on the blanket next to his son and traced one finger along the scar. It had healed but was still pink and looked tender, but Ben didn't react to Jordan touching it. "He couldn't have understood what was happening to him."

"No," Cory agreed. "But at some level he had to know it was a huge trauma. He fought for his life, Jordan, and he survived. Your son is a survivor. I know you think he's fragile, which in some ways all babies are. But he's tough, too. Think about his strength and determination instead of his size or that he's helpless." She crouched down next to Jordan and kissed the top of the boy's head. "I think he gets a lot of that strength from his father."

When their gazes met, hers was tender. Once again, she seemed to understand exactly what Jordan needed to hear—reassuring him both that the baby was strong and that Jordan had a place in his life. He didn't understand how Kade had let her go. The guy might have a hell of a throwing arm, but otherwise he was a complete fool.

With her so close that he could feel her breath against his face, it seemed the most natural thing in the world to lean in and brush a gentle kiss across her sweet mouth. It was different from the way he'd kissed her at the bar. This was a vow, a quiet promise that they were in this together. It was a question about what they could mean to each other if they tried.

A question that was answered when Cory pulled away so fast she fell on her bottom, then scrambled to her feet.

"I'm sorry," he said immediately, even though he didn't regret kissing her. He couldn't regret it.

She pressed two fingers to her lips as if his touch had burned her. "I need to go. The instructions are written on the paper on the counter. Call if there's a problem."

"Cory, I didn't mean to upset you." Jordan made to stand, but she held out a hand.

"It's fine. I'm fine." She flashed a wan smile. "Have a fun boys' night in." With a last look at Ben, she hurried from the room.

"A customer at table five wants to talk to the chef."

Cory looked up from where she was chopping a celery stalk two hours later as the waitress, Misty, ducked her head like she thought the boss might throw something at her.

Cory didn't blame her. Madison didn't speak to her staff as much as she did growl and command. She rarely raised her voice but didn't need to. Her rigid tone reminded Cory of a military commander—one who wouldn't tolerate being questioned.

Cory had discovered that the hard way when she'd asked a series of questions about how the different menu items were prepped. Madison had looked at her like she was the biggest fool on the planet. Cory wasn't sure what it said about her that she didn't flinch in the face of so much silent condemnation. If the surly chef was trying to chasten Cory, she'd have to work a lot harder. Cory'd grown up with a mother who enjoyed tearing her down for sport. She could handle almost anything.

The same couldn't be said for Misty, who'd told Cory she'd taken the part-time waitressing job while attending a nearby university. Misty was the first in her family to attend college and wanted to give her parents a little relief on tuition by making extra money.

Cory knew what it was like to work to put herself through school, so she admired the younger woman's dedication. Actually, Misty was only a few years younger than Cory, although Cory felt decades older. But Misty had also confided that she was thinking of looking for work elsewhere just so she didn't have to deal with the woman who ran the kitchen.

"Why?" Madison's eyes narrowed as she pointed a spatula at the waitress. "What did you do?"

"N-nothing," Misty stammered.

"Are they complaining about the food?"

"I'm not sure. It's a woman. She seems happy enough. Maybe she wants to pay her compliments to the chef."

"The chef doesn't need or want compliments."

"I'll go." Cory wiped her hands on a towel and stepped out from behind the counter. "I can accept a compliment on your behalf and explain that the chef is so humble and shy she doesn't like to leave the kitchen."

Misty smothered a burst of laughter as Madison glared at Cory. "I don't have a shy bone in my body."

"Or a heart," Chuck, the other line cook, called from where he was deep-frying wings at the far side of the kitchen.

Cory saw the briefest instant of pain in Madison's blue gaze before she shuttered it again. "My heart goes into the food. I don't bother sucking up to customers," she shot back, then flicked her fingers at Cory. "See what Ms. High-Maintenance wants. If she complains or asks for a comped meal, dump a beer on her."

"Interesting tactic," Cory said as she headed for the front of the bar. "But I think I can handle this. Point me to table five," she told Misty.

The bar was even more crowded than last night. She liked the energy of the place, groups of people together laughing and having fun.

Tanya, who was tending bar on her own tonight, gave her a questioning gaze as she walked by. Cory waved and smiled, then placed a hand on Misty's arm. "You're doing a good job handling Madison," she told her.

"She's awful." Misty shook her head. "I know she cooks great food, but is it worth it?"

"Have you tried the fried cheese?" Cory sighed. "It will change your world."

"I heard you were Jordan's fiancée," Misty said as she glanced at Cory. "You must be titanium strong. He's scary, too."

"Jordan?" Cory chuckled. "Nah, he's a big teddy bear."

Misty snorted, then pointed to a two-topper in the corner. "That's her. I'm sorry I didn't figure out what she wants. I got flustered when she said she wanted to talk to the chef, knowing I'd have to ask Madison to come out."

"It's fine." Cory approached the woman with a smile. She'd worked at a diner just off campus all four years of school. There was no customer complaint or irritation she couldn't handle.

"Hi, I'm Cory. Is there something I can help you with?"

"You aren't the chef." The woman frowned at her. She had long, wavy brown hair and was dressed in a bulky cable-knit sweater and leggings. She looked comfortable and still stylish, with understated diamond hoops in her ears. Cory guessed she either had or came from money.

"No," Cory agreed. "I'm one of the sous-chefs." To be honest, she didn't exactly know what that meant, but it sounded better than glorified slave in the kitchen. "The head chef is in the middle of something, so if I can be of assistance—"

"I need a recipe." The woman pointed to her bowl of beer-braised chicken stew, of which there were only two bites left. "This recipe, to be specific."

"I'm not sure that's how it works at a restaurant." Cory had watched in awe earlier as Madison toasted anise seeds and then blended them in a food processor with a variety of other spices, bathing the kitchen in their heavenly aroma. She'd put together the seemingly simple chicken dish, tonight's special, in a way that seemed effortless but would have been impossibly demanding to a chef with lesser talent.

The woman shook her head and narrowed her hazel eyes. "Trophy Room isn't a restaurant. It's a local dive bar that happens to currently serve the best food I've had on three continents." She held out a hand. "I'm Ella Samuelson. I grew up in Starlight, and I guarantee you can't get a meal like this anywhere else in town."

"We're glad you like it, but I highly doubt the chef will share her recipes. What would keep you coming back?"

Ella's jaw set in a hard line. "You don't understand. I have to cook something this amazing in two days. It's imperative."

"Why?" Cory asked, and Ella frowned.

"The reason is private."

"So is the recipe."

Ella closed her eyes for a moment and drew in a deep breath. "I have a friend coming to town. Toby doesn't think I can cook. He doesn't think I can do anything remotely wifeish."

"Is that a bad thing?" Cory asked, genuinely curious.

"He sees me as one of the guys," Ella said, her shoulders slumping slightly. "We worked together."

"Doing what?"

"I'm a nurse. I was a nurse. I'm not anymore."

"You're the woman Mara mentioned," Cory murmured. "Her friend who works as a nanny."

"Sometimes," Ella admitted, almost sheepishly. "I'm trying to figure out what my next move is going to be."

"And you want to put the moves on your former coworker?"

"That sounds pathetic." Ella scooped up another bite of chicken. "But maybe. Can you get me the recipe?"

Cory opened her mouth to say no, then had an idea. "I might be able to if you join our cooking club."

Ella blinked. "I gave up clubs in middle school."

"Don't be silly." Cory clapped her hands together. "It will be great."

"I just need a recipe to make before my friend gets here."

"Are you normally a good cook?"

"I've been a traveling nurse for the past five years. Cooking skills weren't much of a priority for me."

"Then learning to cook the dish will be the perfect start."

"By Saturday?" Ella looked skeptical.

"Our first meeting is this week in the Trophy Room kitchen."

"Jordan is letting you use his bar for your club?"

Cory laughed, hoping it sounded casual and not manic. "I'm his fiancée. He can hardly say no."

"And the chef will agree to teach me?"

"All of us," Cory said, nodding.

"How many of us are there?"

"Well, just you and me for now. But Madison's reputation is huge in Starlight."

"Her reputation or her food's reputation? They aren't the same thing."

"Do you want to learn how to make the dish or not?" Cory glanced over her shoulder. She was going out on a limb. In fact, she half expected Madison to come charging out of the kitchen to see what was taking her so long.

"I'll be here to learn to cook."

"You have to commit to four meetings. Twice a month."

"Are you making this up as you go along?"

"Maybe."

"I respect your honesty. Two months of a cooking club. If things work out this weekend with Toby, I'll need more than one recipe."

"Yay."

"Don't say 'yay.' You sound like you're twelve."

Ella handed Cory her cell phone. "Text me the details and I'll be there."

Cory clasped her hand to her chest as she turned back toward the kitchen. For a person who didn't like to lie or be assertive, she was certainly turning over a new leaf in Starlight.

It was a leaf she quite liked.

Chapter Nine

"Thanks for coming," Jordan told Josh Johnson as he stepped back to let the local contractor into his home. Josh had done some work at the bar, and he was Mara's brother-in-law plus a Starlight native. Although everyone in town was a fan of Josh's easygoing nature, Jordan didn't know him well. He'd been somewhat surprised at Josh's willingness to help with the project Jordan had planned.

"I have insane painting skills," Josh answered, holding up a bucket filled with brushes and rollers. "My employees are going to love having a staff appreciation happy hour at the bar. That woman you hired is a unicorn in the kitchen. Everything she makes tastes like sunshine and roses." He grimaced.

"Although, I saw her the other day in the grocery and tried to give her a compliment about the mango salsa she served with her fish tacos. She practically ripped my head off."

"She's working on her people skills," Jordan admitted. "She has a ways to go on the lessons."

"Yeah. She scared the hell out of me. I thought chefs liked compliments."

"I'm not sure we've discovered anything Madison likes other than cooking." Jordan tried not to let frustration seep into his tone. As amazing as his chef's skills in the kitchen were, her attitude was becoming a problem. If her temper and surly demeanor overshadowed her food, he was going to have to make a change. Or convince her to make a change. Maybe Cory and her never-ending supply of positivity could help with that.

All she'd said when she came home from her first shift was that it had been "fun," and then she'd checked on Ben and gone straight to bed. Jordan didn't know if she was exhausted or simply intent on ignoring him after he'd made the mistake of kissing her for real yesterday.

He still couldn't bring himself to regret it, but he also couldn't stop thinking about her softness and how good it felt to be that close to her.

"Did you get the paint?" Josh asked, pulling Jordan from his thoughts.

"Two gallons of natural, nontoxic paint. Thanks for the recommendation."

"Of course. A couple guys from my crew are on their way. Let's get any furniture moved out of the room, and we should be able to knock this job out in an hour."

"Perfect. Cory said she'd be back before Ben's nap time at one, and I'd love to surprise her with a finished nursery."

"I have some stuff I saved from when Anna was a baby, too. We were surprised about the sex, so everything's neutral in color. It will make the room look finished, at least until Cory does her own decorating. Do you want to tell me about the new fiancée?"

"I'm a dad," Jordan said simply.

"I got that with the request for help painting a nursery." Josh followed Jordan through the house. "Apparently, you're also going to be a husband. There's keeping things close to the vest, and there's being downright spy-worthy secretive."

"It's more complicated than that. I don't feel like I can say much else, other than I'm going to do my best to be a good father. Maybe you can give me lessons, because I don't know the first thing about it, and you're an expert."

"Hardly," Josh said with a laugh. He was a big bear of a man, an inch or so taller than Jordan, with light brown hair that looked like it hadn't been trimmed in months and at least two days' worth of stubble darkening his jaw. He was dressed in a long-sleeve Henley and tan work pants, which Jordan imagined was his standard contractor uniform. "The most important part is showing up every day. I know that for sure. Everything else you can figure out as you go. Kids are resilient. Anna taught me that. She's way tougher than I could have ever been."

Jordan had moved to town shortly after Josh's young daughter, Anna, had been diagnosed with leukemia. Apparently, Josh's wife had left Starlight and divorced Josh, unable to handle having a sick child. So Josh and Anna had managed through her chemo treatments together, and she was now a precocious and healthy kindergartner.

Jordan spent time with Josh when he occasionally came into the bar for lunch with his brother, Parker, and a couple of Parker's friends, police chief Nick Dunlap and Finn Samuelson, whose family ran the local bank. Jordan had never heard him complain about being a single father or the added responsibility. Anna was the center of his world, something Jordan hadn't been able to understand until Cory and Ben came into his life.

As they moved the crib and dresser into Jordan's bedroom, Josh continued to give little tidbits of parenting advice while asking subtle questions about Cory and Jordan's relationship. Jordan hadn't thought about how much to share of the details of his son's trauma but figured if anyone could understand, it would be Josh.

"Ben had heart surgery when he was less than a week old," he said as they spread drop cloths over the floor.

"Are you serious?"

He looked up to find Josh staring at him, wide-eyed. "Yeah. They had to fix a narrow valve. It was critical." Bile rose in his throat like it did every time he thought of Cory and Ben facing that trauma on their own.

"He's okay now?"

Jordan nodded.

"Then why don't you look okay?"

"It's hard for me to talk about or even think about what he went through," Jordan admitted. "And what his condition could mean down the road. He's healthy now, but what if that changes? What if I can't protect him?"

"Oh man." Josh scrubbed a hand over his face. "If I had a nickel for every time I worried about Anna's future, I'd have a lot of nickels. One of the biggest lessons cancer taught me was there are no guarantees on anything. Anna will see the oncologist annually for scans, and I can't imagine ever sleeping a full night in the week leading up to her appointment. The relief I feel when she gets a clean report is indescribable."

"How do you deal with it?" Jordan asked, genuinely curious about a father's point of view. "I don't want to talk to Cory about my fears. She doesn't need to deal with my anxiety when I'm sure she's got plenty of her own. I should be the strong one."

Josh blew out a breath. "And you think being the dad means you can never show any emotion? Let me guess—you learned that lesson from your old man."

"Pretty much," Jordan admitted.

"Mine was the same way," Josh said, "although he had a mile-long mean streak when he drank. Parker was better at not letting anything faze him, or at least he had a better poker face than I did. My dad saw me as weak because of it."

"My dad saw me as a way to finally live out his own dreams of sports fame. I was his second chance, and I still resent the hell out of it."

"Do you want to be like your dad?"

"Not in any way."

"Then don't." Josh shrugged. "That part is easy."

"None of it feels easy," Jordan said. "Although, Cory makes being a mom look so natural."

"Then you're lucky. Don't make her handle parenting alone." Josh gestured to the empty bedroom. "All it takes is a little work to make your future into something special."

"You're like the Dr. Phil of contractors," Jordan said with a laugh. "Do you charge extra for the life advice?"

"On the house this time."

They both turned as the doorbell rang. "That's my crew," Josh said, patting Jordan on the shoulder as he walked by. "Let's make your boy a nursery."

"Maybe ordering food and putting it in a pan so I could pretend it was my own would have been easier." Ella glanced at Cory, who tried for a reassuring smile.

Both of them winced as another crash came from the Trophy Room kitchen. After her conversation with Ella, Cory had returned to the kitchen with the goal of convincing Madison to agree to the idea of a cooking club. It had taken a lot of cajoling and begging, but the chef had finally said a reluctant yes. She hadn't seemed happy about it, but Cory figured a bit of time would soften her attitude.

Instead, Madison had stormed into the bar fifteen minutes earlier, complaining loudly and with an impressive stream of curses about wasting her morning off. She'd told both the women that they would have to wait until she got things set up in the kitchen, because she wasn't going to be slowed down by two amateurs.

"She'll be fine once we get started on the recipe," Cory said, then turned as the front door to the bar opened, sunlight streaming into the empty space. She certainly hoped it wasn't Jordan, because she didn't need to hear another round of I-told-you-so about whether Madison could play well with others.

"Is this the cooking class?" a petite woman asked as she stepped into the bar. Her timid voice was at odds with her flaming-red hair. "I saw a flyer posted over at the coffee shop this morning. Is it too late to join?"

Cory felt her mouth open and shut in surprise. "It's not too late." She jumped out of her chair and moved forward, holding out a hand. "Your timing is perfect. We were just about to get started. We're calling it a cooking club. But the Trophy Room chef will be teaching the rest of us."

Another crash, this one louder than the last.

"Oh yes," Ella said, shaking her head. "This is shaping up to be a ton of fun."

Ben gave a soft cry when the pacifier slipped from his mouth. Ella immediately bent down to unstrap him from the infant seat and lift him into her arms. "I'm totally using your baby as a shield."

"Why does she need a shield for a cooking class?" the redhead asked, eyeing the door to the kitchen warily.

"It's a joke." Cory smiled at the woman. "I'm Cory Hall. The cooking club was my idea, although I'm not teaching it. I want to learn to cook."

"She's got a hot fiancé to impress," Ella called out.

"Not really." Cory shook her head, then frowned. "I mean, he's hot, but I'm not trying to impress him."

"I'm trying to impress a guy." Ella lifted Ben

above her head, and he kicked excitedly as he took in his elevated view.

"I don't have a guy to impress," the new woman admitted, sounding a little disappointed. "Is that part of the deal with this club? Women trying to impress men?"

"Not a bit," Cory assured her. "I'm actually new to town and wanted to meet some other women. What's your name?"

"Oh." The flame-haired beauty ducked her head like she was embarrassed that she'd forgotten to introduce herself. "I'm Tessa Reynolds. I'm new to town, too. My aunt had a cabin here that I moved into a couple of weeks ago. I work from home, so I haven't had a chance to meet very many people. That's part of why I wanted to learn to cook. I also just need an excuse to get out of the house."

"I grew up here, so I know everyone," Ella announced, turning Ben around in her lap.

"So you have a lot of friends in town already?" Tessa asked.

"I know people," Ella clarified. "Which is different than having friends. I don't want friends."

"Everyone wants friends," Cory argued.

"I definitely do," Tessa said, almost under her breath.

"I don't want friends."

All three of them turned toward the kitchen, as Madison came through the swinging door and crossed her arms over her chest. "And it feels like a colossal waste of time to teach a trio of losers how to boil water."

Ella snorted. "We aren't losers."

"You can boil water in the microwave," Tessa said.

"I don't use a microwave," Madison answered with a dismissive sniff. "I've never found a use for one."

Cory found that hard to believe. Her mother had heated up a wide array of frozen foods in the microwave and taught Cory to fend for herself with the ubiquitous kitchen appliance from a young age. Heaven help her if she'd eaten the last Lean Cuisine pizza when her mom went looking for an easy dinner.

"Jordan was impressed you agreed to be part of our cooking club." The lie rolled off Cory's tongue so smoothly she wondered if she should be worried at how effortless it was becoming to not tell the truth. She'd always believed without question in the importance of the truth. "He thinks it will be good for your image and great PR for the bar."

"Stop calling it a club," Ella demanded even as she snuggled Ben closer. "I told you I'm not a joiner. We're taking a class."

"I like the idea of a club." Tessa tucked a long strand of hair behind her ear. "Do any of you play Bunco?"

"No," the other three women answered in unison.

"My mom had a great Bunco group," the redhead

shared. "I used to watch when the women were over. I could teach you all if you want."

"Let's get through one meeting at a time," Cory advised gently.

"Right."

Madison glanced at her watch. "I've got two hours before I'm leaving, so if we're going to do this, we need to get started. No messing around." She pointed a long finger at Ben. "And no babies. I don't like babies."

"I love babies," Tessa said. "He's adorable."

"Ben stays," Cory told the chef, hands on her hips. "Unless you want me to call Jordan and tell him you hate his son."

Madison narrowed her eyes, then turned on her heel and stalked back to the kitchen.

"Well played," Ella said, straightening from her chair. "You look like a wimp, but you've got moxie."

"Thank you, I think." Cory shook her head.

"Moxie is a compliment," Tessa told her. "Do you want me to take him?" She held out her hands toward the baby.

Ella shook her head. "Human shield, remember. She can't hurt me if I'm behind the baby."

Tessa looked genuinely shocked. "Is she going to hurt one of us?"

Madison leaned around the kitchen door. "She is if you all don't get your butts into the kitchen so we can get started."

* * *

"I take back every mean thing I said to you."

Madison arched a brow at Ella, who was forking up bites of the baked pasta dish like she hadn't eaten in days. "You didn't say anything mean," Madison told her.

"Maybe they were just mean thoughts," Ella admitted. "But never mind. All is forgiven thanks to this amazing food."

Cory quickly clinked a fork against her water glass. "A toast to our amazing instructor. Thank you for taking the time to teach us how to make this dish."

"If Toby doesn't want more than friendship after this," Ella said, shaking her head, "he might not be the one after all."

They sat around one of the tables toward the back of Trophy Room, four women with little in common but an unspoken need for companionship and an appreciation for great food. The sausage and broccoli rabe dish they'd made seemed simple, but the flavors were complex and multilayered. It was truly the best pasta Cory had ever eaten.

After a less than auspicious start, Cory had been concerned that she'd made a huge mistake in bringing together the group. But once they got into the kitchen, Madison relaxed into her element. Even Ben seemed fascinated watching the talented chef work her magic. Between sautéing the vegetables and adding fresh herbs to the dish, Cory, Ella and Tessa had followed her instructions to the letter.

Tessa had pulled a pad of paper out of her tote bag and taken copious notes on each section of the recipe. She'd promised to transcribe and distribute them to the other two, which Ella had definitely appeared to appreciate, since she was going to try to re-create the dish for her potential boyfriend.

Cory thought things might get tense again once they were all around the table, but the pleasure of the food mellowed each of them.

"Why do you want a guy who's put you in the friend zone anyway?" Madison asked, tipping her glass toward Ella. "It's not like you're horrible to look at, and you seem to have an okay personality— a little annoying, but nothing out of the ordinary."

Ella blinked at the backhanded compliment.

"Moxie was better." Tessa turned to Ella. "But she does have a point."

"You don't understand the pressure we were under when we met. We were in a combat zone working to vaccinate children in rural villages against a measles outbreak. There was no time for anything but friendship. We were too busy keeping kids alive."

"That's a huge responsibility and must have taken an amazing amount of commitment," Cory said quietly. "So why aren't you working in nursing now that you're back in Starlight? Trust me, I'm not complaining. If you can help out with Ben a couple nights a week, it would be just a godsend for me. I can't imagine anyone more qualified to take care of my baby."

"I need a break," Ella said simply. "Plus I'm not sure whether I'm going to stay in town long term."

"This place is amazing." Tessa dabbed a napkin at the corner of her mouth. "Anyone would want to live here."

"It's a little off the beaten path," Madison noted. "Certainly isn't the easiest place to find really fresh ingredients."

"I think it's perfect." Tessa grinned. "And now I have friends, which makes it even more perfect. I've never been part of a club before."

"You aren't now," the chef told her. "I taught you all to cook something impressive because this one—" she pointed at Cory "—has influence with the boss. Somehow I've gotten the reputation of having a bad attitude."

"I can't imagine why," Ella muttered dryly.

Madison sniffed. "If you get some action from making my recipe, you won't care about my attitude."

"I don't care about it now." Ella shrugged. "I'd rather you be grumpy than fake nice." She bit down on her lower lip. "My dad and brother seem to think there's something wrong with me because I came home and didn't immediately jump back into nursing. Like I'm fragile and need them to coddle me."

"I hate being coddled," Tessa said, and the bitterness in her tone shocked Cory. The redhead had seemed like a regular Pollyanna before this moment.

Madison and Ella seemed just as surprised. All three of them stared at Tessa until she shifted uncomfortably under their scrutiny.

"Spill it," Madison commanded. "I can tell you have a story to share."

"No." Tessa fidgeted.

Madison tapped a finger on the tabletop, and no one spoke.

"I had a kidney transplant two years ago," Tessa blurted. "It's not a big deal."

Ella pointed a finger in her direction. "In fact, a new organ is a big deal."

"I'm fine now. I take my medicine every day, and my health is better than it's ever been. But my parents treat me like blown glass, as if I'll shatter under the slightest pressure. It's why I moved to Starlight. I had to get away. I was suffocating." She drew in a shaky breath. "I'm creating a new life here. One that I live on my terms."

"That makes two of us," Madison said, offering a surprisingly gentle smile.

"Me three," Ella added.

"It's official." Cory drew in a shaky breath. "We're a club."

"Yes." Tessa pumped her fist in the air.

Ella shrugged. "I guess hanging with you all is

less pathetic than spending every night with my dad and his girlfriend."

They all looked toward Madison. "Fine," she grumbled. "I'll teach you all to cook for your little club. We're also going to have some ground rules. I'm willing to do it twice a month like Cory suggested, but not here every time. You all are going to have to open up your kitchens. I have a reputation to protect as a professional."

"Actually, I think your reputation is something you need to fix," Cory reminded her. "At least the customer-service part."

"So we're doing you a favor," Ella said, then smothered a laugh when Madison threw her a dirty look.

"Chop It Like It's Hot." Tessa nodded. "That's our name."

"You're joking," Madison muttered.

"I like it." Cory grinned at Tessa. "Every good club needs a name."

Madison sniffed. "I've changed my mind."

"No take backs," Tessa said in a firm tone.

Even Madison couldn't hide her grin at that. They finished the meal and cleaned up the kitchen until no one would be able to tell anyone had been there. Ben began to fuss and rub his eyes, a sure sign that the baby was ready for his nap.

Cory exchanged numbers with the women before heading back to Jordan's house, hope blooming in her chest for the first time in ages. The idea of no take backs tumbled through her mind. So far she didn't want to take back a single thing about her decision to come to Starlight. She sent up a silent prayer of gratitude to her grandmother. This truly felt like starting over, and Cory was one step closer to creating a life she could be proud of.

Chapter Ten

Jordan met Cory at the door of his house, a nervous smile playing around the corners of his mouth.

"How was your cooking class?" he asked, stepping back into the entry to let her pass.

"I brought you lunch." She held up the take-home box of leftovers. "Madison is truly talented."

"Yeah," he agreed, scratching his jaw. "I just hope that will be reason enough to keep her around despite the attitude." He reached out a hand for the infant carrier. "Let me take him."

Cory tried not to look stunned. This might have been the first time Jordan had offered to take the baby from her. Not that he wasn't willing to pitch in when she asked, but he still seemed too uncomfortable to do it on his own, even though he'd stayed with Ben during her first shift at Trophy Room without incident.

"You can't fire her," Cory said simply. "She's actually quite nice."

Jordan arched a brow. "Right. She's cuddly like a grizzly bear."

"She's working on it," Cory insisted. "I'm helping her."

"You barely know her."

"She gave me a job. I owe her."

Ben interrupted whatever Jordan was going to say with a loud cry.

"Did I do something wrong?" Jordan immediately placed the carrier on the counter and took a step back like he'd hurt the baby.

"He's tired. A nap will make everything better."

"Right." Jordan unclipped the boy from the seat and lifted him out. Ben whimpered and rubbed his face against the soft fabric of Jordan's T-shirt. "About that…"

Cory frowned. "About a nap?"

"I have something to show you."

"That sounds ominous."

"It seemed like a good idea at the time," Jordan said cryptically. "Now I'm not sure. If you don't like it, I can make any changes you want. I probably should have waited or gotten your opinion, but—"

"Show me." Cory put a hand on his arm, unsure

whether to be amused or alarmed by his sudden case of nerves. This was a new side of Jordan, one that was strangely appealing. Other than with Ben, he always seemed so sure of himself. She'd envied that confidence back in Atlanta, where she'd spent the better part of her life second-guessing every decision she made.

She followed him through the house toward the hallway that led to the bedrooms. When he flipped on a light in the spare room where they'd set up the crib, Cory gasped and placed a hand to her chest.

In the few hours she'd been gone, the space had been transformed into a soothing sanctuary. Instead of plain beige walls, the room was now painted a soft sage green that reminded her of Ben's eyes when he woke in the morning. Two free-floating wooden shelves hung next to the crib, and a new bookcase sat on the other side of a wooden rocking chair.

"What did you do?" she whispered, awed by the transformation.

"I figured Ben needed a real room before my mom arrives," Jordan told her, his big hand rubbing gentle circles on the baby's back as he held him. A faint blush colored his cheeks, and the image of this giant man blushing made her heart skip a beat. "A friend of mine in construction came over with a couple of guys from his crew, so it only took about thirty minutes to do the walls. I made sure to get the natural, nontoxic paint, so there are no fumes."

"I can't even smell it," Cory confirmed. She brushed away the sudden tears that sprang to her eyes. "It's perfect."

"Then why are you crying?" Jordan asked quietly. "I don't want you to cry, Cory."

"Happy tears," she said with a watery laugh. "Ignore them."

Ben gave another cry, arching his back and rubbing his eyes.

"He's going to sleep so well in his new room."

"Josh told me that he'd be fine in here because it's environmentally safe paint. If you're not comfortable, we can move the crib."

"Lay him down, Jordan." Cory tried to keep the emotion from her voice.

As Cory turned off the overhead light and closed the shades, Jordan placed the baby in the crib, which was now covered with a striped sheet that matched the throw pillow on the rocking chair.

Ben fussed for a brief second before relaxing to sleep.

His own room, decorated specifically for him. Something she'd only dreamed of providing for him.

She kept her gaze averted as she led the way back to the family room, still trying not to reveal how much the gesture affected her. As if her tears weren't a giveaway.

Her legs felt like jelly, so she lowered herself to the sofa and took a deep, hopefully calming breath.

"You should really eat the pasta before it gets cold. Even I'm amazed I could make something that tastes so good."

"Did I mess up with the paint?" Jordan sat down next to her, so close that his leg brushed hers, sending awareness shivering all the way to her toes. "You've been dealing with so much for Ben. Everything, in fact, and it's amazing. You're an amazing mom, Cory. I just wanted to play a part. Stinky diapers might not be my comfort level, but I can slap on a coat of paint with the best of them. Like I said, if you want to change it, that's fine. I'll have the guys back out here tomorrow."

Now she felt like an even bigger jerk for making him feel bad when he'd made such a wonderful gesture. Yet Cory still didn't trust herself to speak without losing it completely. The last thing she wanted was to burst into loud, hiccuping sobs. If Jordan wasn't freaked out by her behavior already, that would do the trick.

Instead of using words, she did the only thing she felt capable of in the moment. She wrapped her fingers around his large, calloused hand and lifted it to her mouth, pressing a kiss to his knuckles. And then another and another, ignoring that her tears were slowly dripping all over both of them.

Cory didn't like to cry.

After Ben's birth, when the shock of having him whisked away overwhelmed her, she'd given in to one night of self-indulgent weeping. She'd spent hours in her hospital bed crying until she had no more tears inside her, then dry heaving over a hospital basin as the medicine from her C-section moved through her body and she tried to process her new reality. But that was it. After that night, she'd met with the doctors and begun the process of figuring out how to best help her precious boy, even when she felt helpless. She stayed positive in the face of whatever life handed her.

In some ways, it felt as if she'd poured out all of her tears and had nothing left to give. Even in the last few difficult weeks of her grandmother's life and at the funeral. Or when her mother had callously informed Cory she had two days to vacate her gran's house. Although tiny and cramped, it was the only home Ben had ever known. His crib had been shoved against the wall in the spare bedroom, and Cory had slept on an old twin mattress with no box spring only a few feet from him.

Sometimes late at night when she couldn't sleep, she'd hack into the Wi-Fi of the couple next door and spend hours looking at houses on the internet. Homes with bright white kitchens and family rooms with vaulted ceilings and stone fireplaces. Master suites with beds so big they looked like they could fit an army of people, and nurseries that felt like harbingers of a happy childhood.

She'd lived in a huge house in Atlanta with Kade,

but his taste had been modern and streamlined to the point it felt sterile. Her closet had been filled with clothes he'd picked up for her, and she'd had no say in any part of their home. She would have slept on that twin mattress for her entire life if the alternative was giving up so much of herself for a man's whims and desires.

Jordan had decorated that room for Ben, but Cory was the one shattered by his thoughtfulness. She'd spent so long being strong and pretending like nothing fazed her, but what she hadn't been able to give her son festered like a wound that wouldn't heal. It stung at odd times, forcing her to block out the pain so she could keep going.

The simple act of creating a real space for Ben in his home had simultaneously helped to heal her and created a new, deeper cut across her heart. It brought her to her knees.

"You're killing me," he whispered, his voice rough with pain. "They don't seem like happy tears, Cory. Please don't cry."

How could she explain what he'd unleashed inside her when she barely understood it herself? She lifted her gaze to his, ready to do her best, but the intensity in his brilliant green eyes unlocked another layer of the defenses she'd built around her heart.

Without thinking about the consequences—Lord, she was so sick of thinking—she leaned in and kissed him. Purposefully and with an open mouth, not wanting him to mistake her meaning. This wasn't an accidental brush of the lips or her being swept up in the moment. The emotion pounding through her demanded a release, and this was the only way she knew to relieve the pressure.

Their breath mingled, and Jordan groaned low in his throat, as if her touch was as painful to him as her tears. But when she started to pull back, not wanting to make him uncomfortable, he cupped her cheeks in his big hands and shifted closer.

The kiss deepened, warm and wet, and Cory hummed her pleasure against his lips. He overwhelmed her senses, his soapy scent swirling around them and the scratch of his stubble at odds with the impossible softness of his lips. Cory gave herself completely to the moment, to the desire that blotted out everything until she couldn't even remember her own name.

The longer they kissed, the less she felt anything but the deep satisfaction of his mouth against hers, his hands cradling her like she was something precious. No anger or guilt or worry could push its way through the bubble of desire that surrounded them. This might not be real, but it was now and it was everything.

So when he pulled her closer, it felt like the most natural thing ever for Cory to climb into his lap and press herself against him. His hands squeezed her arms and she moved her hips, just enough to feel that he was as moved by her as she was by him.

The realization only fueled the fire that had started deep inside her.

"Cory." His voice rasped against her jaw as she ran her fingers through his messy hair.

"Are you reminding yourself who you're with?" She tugged at the soft strands.

"I could never forget." As if to prove it, he took her mouth again, a claiming more than an exploration. One she wanted with her whole being.

She grabbed the hem of his T-shirt, lifting it up and over his head. So much heat emanated from him, and she'd been frozen for so long.

Of course, she'd seen his body before. Hard planes and six-pack abs that distracted her from the simple task of breathing. She'd seen plenty of athletes without their shirts on at the pool parties Kade liked to throw during the hellish heat of summer in Georgia. But Jordan was different. This moment felt different.

It felt as if he belonged to her, even though it was only temporary and mostly pretend. Completely pretend, she reminded herself, but even that didn't dull her desire the way she'd expected. Not when he seemed content to give her whatever she needed, like he understood she was a stick of dynamite and he held the match.

She ran her palms across the dark hair that covered his skin. His heart beat a frantic pace, and she could see his chest rise and fall in shallow breaths. It felt essential that she taste his skin, so she kissed the place where his clavicle dipped at the base of his throat. He rewarded her with a low groan, and she kissed his mouth again.

He tasted like all the things she'd convinced herself she shouldn't want, not when her priority was Ben. As if sensing the emotions warring inside her, he gentled their connection, but Cory didn't want gentle. She wanted to escape for a few minutes, to forget about everything but the way her body felt pressed to his.

"More," she whispered against his lips, and bless him, he gave it to her. The air around them was filled with their wanting.

Her shirt was gone in an instant, and her skin felt hot everywhere he touched. She wanted him everywhere.

He rose from the sofa, lifting her in his arms like she weighed nothing. They continued to kiss as he carried her through the house, and she laughed softly at his ability to walk without running into anything. Cory wasn't sure it was a feat she'd be able to manage.

"Normally women don't laugh when I'm taking them to my bed," he said, his voice hoarse.

"Do you make a habit of taking women to your bed?" she asked, then immediately regretted it. Did she really want to know about the other potential women in his life? He didn't owe her anything, but the thought of Jordan with someone else made jealousy spike inside her.

He paused at his bedroom's threshold, pulling back enough to look into her eyes. "No." His gaze was clear on hers. "There have been no women in this house, Cory. Only you."

Well, if that didn't just slay her.

She wrapped her arms more tightly around him and nipped at his earlobe. There was no way she was going to allow him to see what those words meant to her.

The room was furnished with a bed and dresser crafted from some type of reclaimed barn wood, sturdy and clean. It was a perfect reflection of Jordan.

He pulled back the covers and placed her on the soft sheets, his hands smoothing along her torso. His thumbs caught in the waistband of her leggings, and he tugged them, along with her panties, over her hips.

"You're beautiful," he said even as she automatically covered the C-section scar with one hand. His fingers tugged hers away. "Everywhere."

She normally didn't care about the three-inch line across her lower belly. Ben had been born as a result of that incision, and he was worth any trauma her body had to take. But it wasn't exactly a signal of sexy times ahead, although under Jordan's intense gaze, every part of her felt desirable.

"Do you want this, Cory?"

"Yes." She wanted this more than she wanted her next breath. "But you're wearing too many clothes," she teased, needing to keep what was between them light. Hiding what was in her heart.

"Easily remedied." He straightened and shucked off his jeans and boxers, taking a wallet from his back pocket before dropping his pants in a pile on the bedroom floor. He removed a condom from the wallet and then joined her on the bed, warmth radiating from his body like he was her personal space heater. She liked the thought of this man belonging to her, keeping her warm when the world got cold.

It was a fantasy she shouldn't allow herself to entertain, and she pushed all thoughts of the future aside as he settled over her, one knee nudging her legs apart.

Jordan stilled, and their gazes met. She read the question in his eyes. Even now, he was giving her a choice. The recognition of having control moved through her like a cloud of fairy dust, making her feel light-headed with the joy of it.

"Yes," she whispered, unable to put together a more coherent thought.

"Thank God," he said with a rough laugh, his forehead against hers. He took her mouth with his, tongues melding as he pushed inside her. Cory gasped at the pleasure of it, the way her body awakened with longing and recognition.

She could feel the rapid cadence of his breath, like he needed a minute to get himself under control.

But she didn't want control. This wasn't a time for restraint or composure. She wanted to forget everything other than the sensation of the moment, and she didn't want to go there alone.

She skimmed her nails down his back, taking hold of his hips and pressing him closer as she wrapped her legs more tightly around him. They'd only been together once before this, but somehow his body felt familiar to her. He was her perfect fit.

Jordan let out a low moan, and then they moved together, setting a pace that drove her out of her mind in the best way possible. Desire spiked inside her as she realized she couldn't tell where he ended and she began. She held tight to his strong biceps as she arched up to him. Minutes—or hours—later, the pressure built to an erotic peak, and she felt like she might lose herself completely if she didn't get a release from it.

Lose her heart if she wasn't careful.

But it wasn't the time for doubt or reality. Her heart pounded and goose bumps erupted along her skin as Jordan's scratchy jaw traced a path down her neck. His breath was warm on her ear, and he whispered the sweetest words to her. Words that made her feel beautiful and wanted and drove her to the edge of her desire and then over. A thousand sparks broke over her like the bright light of a meteor shower, and a guttural cry tore from her lips.

A moment later, his breath caught and she felt his body tremble with release. She held this big, strong man in her arms as they rode the last waves together, and it was a million times more satisfying than the first time she'd been with him.

Because she wasn't coming to him broken and angry the way she had before. She'd made the choice to give her body to Jordan from a place of power, and that changed everything.

For Cory, this moment changed everything, and that sobering thought was terrifying enough to have her shift under him. She needed to remember the boundaries. The temporary nature of their relationship—the fact that everything between them was pretend.

Except it didn't feel pretend.

The way he dropped gentle kisses in her hair and continued to hold her close. It felt real. It felt like he cared, like she wasn't alone.

Cory hadn't realized how lonely she'd been until the warmth of him reminded her.

But she was still alone. A tumble in the sheets didn't change that, and she couldn't afford to believe it had.

She pushed at his shoulders, and he immediately rolled off her. She sat up and tugged the sheet around her, trying to control her rioting heartbeat.

"What's wrong?"

Jordan's big hand on her back burned like a brand.

"Nothing." She glanced over her shoulder with a patently false smile. "I need to get dressed." How she wished she hadn't left her shirt and bra in the other room. "Thanks for…" She waved a hand toward him, looking ten kinds of a Roman god stretched out next to her on the bed. "I needed that."

"Cory."

"Ella is coming over later this afternoon. She's agreed to watch Ben on the nights we're both working. If your mom wants to stay with him, I guess we can—"

"Cory, stop. Please." His hand moved to her shoulder, and he brushed her hair over to the side before leaning up to kiss her bare skin. "This was more than a physical release. You know that, right? We aren't going to pretend—"

"This is all pretend, Jordan." She yanked the sheet off the bed as she stood and took a step away. "Let's not make more of it than it was. We're two consenting adults, and this was…nice."

"Nice," he repeated with a wince. "I'm losing my touch if you describe the two of us together as nice."

"I don't want to describe anything," she said, fisting her hands in the sheet's soft fabric. "I don't want to talk about this. We have a baby together, and we have to find a way to make things work for his sake. Your mom arrives soon, and your friends—my new friends—think we're a couple. But we're not, Jordan. This is all for show."

He sat up, pulling the comforter over the lower half of his body. "You coming apart under me wasn't pretend." His voice was tight.

"You're right." She shook her head. "Which is why it can't happen again."

"I disagree."

"You don't get a vote."

"Seriously?"

"Please, Jordan. I can't do this right now. I'm working on myself so I don't repeat the mistakes I made in the past."

His mouth pressed into a thin line, but he nodded. "I won't be a mistake for you, and I respect whatever choice you make. For Ben or for yourself. I know this isn't easy."

That was the understatement of the century. She looked down at her painted toes, because if she met his gaze he would see everything she felt. No way she could hide.

"Thank you," she whispered, then backed away and added, "For all of it."

Chapter Eleven

The Friday lunch crowd at the bar was the biggest Jordan had ever seen, although he took little comfort in it. Not with the black mood he'd woken to earlier after a night of tossing and turning and wishing Cory was in his bed and not the guest bedroom down the hall.

He should be thrilled about his full bar. Ever since Madison had started offering a Friday special of fish tacos on the menu, Trophy Room had been slammed from the moment he opened the doors.

There was no denying her expertise with the tacos. The fish, which she had delivered each week from Seattle, was served with a beer-batter coating that she fried to a golden brown and a tender, flaky inside. She accompanied the fish with a homemade slaw and pico de gallo and served the mixture on tortillas made fresh each week by a local woman in town. The bar smelled delicious. Laughter and conversation rang out through the room. When he'd bought the bar, Trophy Room had a been a redneck watering hole that was lucky to have a half dozen customers a night.

He'd transformed the business into something vibrant, a pub he could take pride in that was also part of the community. He'd made this place his home, and it would continue to be no matter what happened with Cory. So why was it so hard to get over her ease in walking away from his bed?

Jordan hadn't lied when he told her that she was the first woman he'd shared it with, but that didn't mean he'd been a monk since moving to Starlight. He preferred the term *discerning*. He dated casually, with women who understood he couldn't offer them more than some mutually beneficial companionship.

Which should make Cory the perfect choice, since she loved to remind him that their arrangement was both temporary and pretend. Yet he couldn't stop thinking about how right it felt to have her in his arms, distracted like he was some lovesick schoolboy. He'd messed up three drink orders in a row, which never happened.

Josh approached the bar after finishing lunch with Parker. The Johnson brothers were Friday regulars, always arriving well before noon since they knew that once the kitchen ran out of fresh fish, the tacos were gone until the following week.

"Have you swapped personalities with your chef?" he asked, arching a thick brow.

Jordan rolled his eyes as irritation filtered through him. Finally, an outlet for all his pent-up frustration. "What are you talking about and what did she do now? I told her that if she didn't adjust her attitude—"

"She personally served our food with a genuine smile." Josh held up a hand to stop Jordan's out-of-character rant. "We even had what one might call a civil conversation. I was shocked."

"Are you sure it was Madison?" Jordan glanced over his shoulder toward the kitchen. "Normally, the waitstaff doesn't let her interact with customers. It's ended badly more than once."

"She brought me extra salsa."

"I don't believe it. She doesn't give extras." A customer at the far end of the bar rapped his knuckles on the countertop to get Jordan's attention. Jordan flicked a glance in the man's direction. "Make a noise like that again, and I'll kick you out of here. I'll be there when I get to you."

He turned back to find Josh grinning at him. "See what I mean? It's like Freaky Friday with you and Chef Maurer. She's sweet as cherry pie, and you're as ornery as a bear coming out of hibernation."

"I'm not ornery."

"Grumpy."

"Or that." Out of the corner of his eye, he saw Tanya take the order of the man he'd just snapped at. "First drink on the house," he called to her.

"Ya think?" she responded.

"How did Cory like the nursery color?" Josh asked.

Jordan's heart clenched as he thought about the emotion that had filled her gaze. "It was good. Thanks again for your help."

"Anytime. I'm having Parker and Mara and her daughter over for a cookout this weekend, if you and Cory want to bring the baby? We try to do a regular Sunday supper a couple times a month."

Jordan blinked. He liked Josh but rarely hung out with people other than when he was behind the bar. It felt strange and somehow nerve-racking to be included, even for a casual get-together.

"My mom comes into town tonight for a visit," he said instead of directly declining.

"Bring her along," Josh said easily. "We might not be cutting-edge fun, but it's family friendly for all generations."

Jordan had barely spoken more than a few sentences to his mom in the past decade. It was difficult to imagine making her part of a social group he wasn't even sure he belonged to.

As if on cue, the door to the street opened, and his mother walked in. He glanced at his watch, because she wasn't supposed to be arriving until closer to dinner.

She patted her neat bob and clutched her purse tight to her side like she was afraid one of his customers might reach out and snatch it from her.

"Appreciate the invite," Jordan told Josh, already moving to the end of the bar. "I'll let you know if we can make it."

Without waiting for a response, he headed toward his mom. It only took a few seconds before she spotted him. He tried to ignore the catch in his heart as her shoulders relaxed and her features gentled.

"Hey, Mom." He stopped in front of her, unsure whether to lean in for a hug or what. His parents had never been demonstrative with affection, and he didn't want to assume that had changed. Although, some quiet place inside him wanted it to.

"Hi," she said, glancing around. "Your bar is crowded for noon. Are there a bunch of alcoholics who live in Starlight?"

He barked out a shocked laugh, then shook his head. So much for considering a hug. "We serve food. Fish-Taco Friday."

"I thought bars served bowls of peanuts or stale popcorn." She swallowed, then glanced up at him. "Do you know this is the first bar I've been to?"

"Since when?"

"My whole life."

"Oh." He thought about how little he truly knew

about his mother and tried for a reassuring smile. "Well, welcome to Trophy Room."

"It smells in here." She sniffed the air. "It smells good, like food."

"Fish tacos," he repeated and led her toward the bar. "Are you hungry? How was your drive? Are you doing okay?"

He wasn't sure how to stem the anxiety that had bloomed inside him or bridge the gap between them. His father had been such a huge presence in their household, it was as if his mother automatically shifted to the shadows. Even now, as they walked past a table, a man scooted his chair out to stand. The edge of the chair bumped her hip, and she recoiled with a gasp.

"You're fine, Mom." Jordan moved behind her, using his body to form a makeshift shield as they moved through the clusters of people. "I've got you."

She smiled a little at that. "You always were a gentleman. I'm sorry if I'm acting like a ninny, Jordie. It's strange to become accustomed to life without your father. One moment I think I'm going to be strong and independent, and the next I realize I'm the same wimp I've always been."

"Mom, you're not a wimp." He rubbed two fingers against his chest. Her use of his childhood nickname hit him square in the solar plexus. "Don't say that." He waved as someone across the room shouted a greeting. "Let's get you some lunch. It was a long drive, and you'll feel better after you eat."

His mother turned to him suddenly. "Are you happy, son?"

And the hits just kept on coming.

"Mostly." He shrugged. "I'm proud of this place and what I've done with it. I know Dad hated when I left football, but it was the right choice for me."

Kathy's gaze focused on him more intently. "Does Cory make you happy?"

"Yes," he answered before he could think better of it. Not that it mattered.

"Tanya." He gestured to the bartender. "This is my mom, Kathy Schaeffer."

"Mrs. Schaeffer, it's nice to meet you." Tanya seemed to have no problem giving his mother a tight squeeze. "It's hard to believe this big oaf came from someone so lovely."

His mom giggled at that. "He was over ten pounds at birth," she said with a nod. "We were convinced I was having twins."

"Ouch." Tanya grimaced at Jordan. "You owe her, buddy. Big-time."

"Yeah," he agreed. "Yeah, I do."

He saw the hitch in his mom's shoulders. There were so many things they needed to talk about if they were finally going to get on the right track. It was difficult to believe that could even happen when he'd started off this new chapter on a lie.

"Why don't you have a seat?" Tanya said to his mom, shooting him a look full of censure when he didn't move. "I'll have the kitchen make up a special plate for you."

He gave himself a mental shake and held the chair still while his mom climbed up into it.

And the scene he never could have imagined—his mom visiting the bar he owned—came to life like it was always meant to be.

Cory was on her hands and knees when she heard the front door open.

Well, knees and one hand, since the other was throbbing in pain and nowhere near able to bear her weight.

Jordan let out a soft curse, and she called out a chipper "It's fine. We're fine" in response. The horrible scent of burned food and the gray plume of smoke coming from the oven told a different story.

She'd opened the windows and turned the vent above the stove on high, but smoke still filled the air.

"What the hell happened?" Jordan asked as he came into the kitchen. He looked completely shocked by the scene in front of him. Cory winced as she sat back on her heels.

"A little mishap with dinner," she said, trying to keep the smile on her face and her voice light. She could feel the wobble in her chin and hated that she'd messed this up, even more so when his mother followed close behind him.

To make a horrible situation even worse, Ben began to whimper from where he sat in his high chair. He'd actually seemed fascinated by the smoke and the mess his mommy made in the kitchen, but now, with an audience, it felt like her baby was throwing her under the bus. As if his cries were voicing what should be clear to all of them—Cory couldn't handle even the simple task of making dinner while taking care of her child.

"Hello, Kathy. I hope you had a good trip." Cory stood and moved toward the high chair. "Sorry about all of this. I'll have it cleaned up in a jiffy."

"A jiffy?" Jordan murmured, his eyes going wide as he looked around at the destruction that included mixing bowls and a sauté pan filling the sink, in addition to the broken casserole dish and food exploded all over the floor.

"Absolutely," Cory answered with more confidence than she felt. She felt no confidence whatsoever. "I have the bed made up for your mom in the guest room, if you want to take her there."

With the embarrassment pouring through her, Cory forgot about the fact that she'd burned her hand grabbing the scorched casserole dish from the oven minutes earlier. She gasped with pain as she put her hands on Ben's torso to lift him up.

Jordan cursed again but moved to her side with

lightning speed and pulled the baby from the high chair. Ben's whimpers turned into full-blown cries.

"Let me take him," Kathy said gently. "I've been looking forward to spending time with my grandson all week." She offered Cory a gentle smile as she took Ben from Jordan's arms. "I can find the bedroom on my own. You get that hand under cold water. Jordan will help you clean up."

She turned and headed for the hallway with Ben's fussing already gentling as she held him close.

Cory wanted to argue. She wanted to apologize again, to both Kathy and Jordan, but was too afraid the sobs she was doing her best to hold back would break free if she tried to speak.

She turned for the sink, but Jordan was already there. He flipped the faucet to cold, held his own hand under to test the temperature and then reached for her.

"I've got it," she whispered.

"You should have had water on that immediately."

She didn't argue because he was right. She also didn't pull away when he took her hand and turned it over to reveal two angry red welts on her fingers.

Out of the corner of one eye, she saw his jaw tighten, but his touch remained gentle. She sucked in a breath when the water sluiced over her skin. "I burned dinner," she said through clenched teeth.

"I don't care about dinner." He didn't take his hand off her wrist, although it was no longer necessary to continue holding her. "You hurt yourself. You have to take care of you."

"I'm fine," she said again, even though it had to be clear that she was anything but okay.

His thumb made circles on the inside of her wrist, the pressure featherlight. "Do you want to tell me about it?"

She shrugged as the water made her skin numb. It was easier to breathe, and she didn't know whether it was the relief from the cold or Jordan's comforting presence next to her.

"Ben went down for a late nap. He woke just as I finished the casserole, so I didn't have time to clean up the kitchen. I put it in the oven and then went to get him."

She pulled her hand out of the stream of water and flipped off the faucet. "Honestly, I lost track of time. It's so stupid. I knew I needed to watch the oven and should have set a timer on my phone." She glanced up at him and grabbed a dish towel from the counter. "He rolled from back to front for the first time. I got distracted."

"It's okay, Cory."

"No." She shook her head. "Moms aren't supposed to get distracted. Babies get hurt. Houses burn down." She broke off and looked away, unable to meet his gaze.

"Cory."

Could he tell this was more than what had happened here this afternoon? She'd wanted this night to prove something, but not like this.

"I wanted to make a good impression on your mom," she said with a soft laugh. "She must think I'm crazy, or at least incompetent."

"Mom will understand. Accidents happen."

She started to bend down again, but Jordan stopped her. "Let's get ointment for your burn. I can handle the cleanup later, and we'll take Mom into town for dinner. She'll like that."

"I hate having you clean up my mess," Cory murmured. "I want to take care of myself."

"You do." He reached out and tucked a strand of hair behind her ear. "Look at how you took care of Ben when he needed you most. I'm still amazed that you managed to handle his surgery and recovery on your own after just giving birth. You're stronger than I could ever imagine."

"You haul kegs around and manage partiers for a living," she reminded him, appreciating his words even if they didn't exactly ring true. She'd only done what any parent would have in the situation. "I bet you could bench-press me."

He flashed a wide grin, stealing her breath in the best way possible. Jordan smiled but not often with this wide, disarming openness. "I could totally bench-press you."

The thought of his hands on her in that way did funny things to her insides. "I'm going to check on your mom and Ben," she said. She looked around him with a frown. "You can leave the kitchen, and I'll clean it later."

"I have aloe in the medicine cabinet under the master bath sink. Take care of your hand and Ben. I'll handle the kitchen, and then we can head out for dinner. We'll make it some place quick and casual, so Ben doesn't get bored."

She bit down on her lower lip, suddenly shy. "I moved my things into the master since your mom is here now."

"That's fine," Jordan said, massaging a hand over the back of his neck. "All part of the plan."

"Yeah," she agreed on a puff of nervous breath.

"Nothing has to happen," he told her. "You made it clear this is just for pretend. Nothing about you and Ben being here is real."

She'd made that clear to him? Good to know, because her mind and heart were a jumbled mess of conflicting emotions. "I appreciate your help with the kitchen." She nodded. That felt like a safe enough conversation. "That's real."

"Okay, then. I should get to it."

Something flashed in his eyes that looked like disappointment. She wasn't the only one who'd agreed to this fake arrangement. Jordan had given her no indication he wanted more.

Unless you counted sex, but Cory didn't. In her experience, men were much better than women at separating physical from emotional intimacy.

She thought about the way he'd held on to her wrist under the faucet, like she was precious to him. Did that count as intimacy? It had certainly felt that way to her.

Unwilling to push him for clarification, she turned and headed toward the bedroom. If he wanted something more from her, he'd tell her. And why would he? Yes, they had Ben in common, but otherwise there was nothing special about her.

She had no career, no college degree and no friends or family looking out for her. She had an old car that probably should be traded in before it conked out completely, all of her worldly possessions fit into a couple of suitcases, and if she lowered her pants, she'd see the iridescent stretch marks that had erupted across her skin during her final trimester of pregnancy, along with the C-section scar.

Oh yes. She was quite the catch.

Plus, she'd burned dinner and practically set his kitchen on fire. First thing tomorrow, she was texting Madison, Tessa and Ella and insisting on another meeting, this one focusing on kitchen basics.

Ella might want to impress a man with a few delectable recipes, but Cory would be happy if she could put an edible dinner on the table without incident. Baby steps, she told herself, then channeled her inner Gran. She could figure this out, she reminded herself. If only she knew how.

Chapter Twelve

"You almost burned down his kitchen? That's hilarious," Ella told Cory the following week as the four unlikely friends met in the small kitchen in Tessa's cabin.

"It's pathetic," Madison said with a sniff. She wore skintight black jeans and a fitted T-shirt fashionably ripped at the collar, looking every inch the force of nature Cory knew her to be. "If you're forgetful, set a timer."

"I meant to." Cory covered her face with her hands. "I forgot."

Tessa patted her shoulder. "It sounds like Jordan was there to save the day."

"I don't want him to save the day," Cory argued.

"I want to be able to save myself. I spent too long feeling indebted to Kade, not to mention all those times growing up when my mom reminded me how choosing to bring me into the world was the beginning of the end as far as her life was concerned."

"A real peach, your mom," Ella said with a grimace.

"She did her best."

Tessa leaned closer. "Sometimes even a person's best can hurt."

"Isn't that the truth," Ella agreed, then turned to Cory. "How is it with Jordan's mom?"

"I like her." Cory smiled. "She's sweet. There's a lot of unspoken tension between the two of them, though. He had problems with his dad growing up, and it seems like that resulted in problems with his mom."

"Families are complicated," Ella murmured.

Madison sniffed. "Families are a pain in the butt. Let's talk food. That's less nauseating. You need to understand some basic techniques that will allow you to make a variety of dishes."

"You also need to learn how to set a timer," Ella told Cory. "That's kind of cooking 101."

"I realize that." Cory shook her head. "It doesn't matter. Once Jordan's mom leaves, it will just be Ben and—" She broke off, remembering that Madison was the only one who knew the truth of her arrangement.

Tessa frowned at her. "Ben will be eating solid food soon enough, and you'll want to cook for Jordan. Or with Jordan."

"Food is love, they say." Ella grimaced. "I don't, actually, and I don't know who 'they' are, but it's a good line."

"It's a ridiculous line," Madison said, pointing a wooden spoon in Ella's direction. "The food itself doesn't have anything to do with love. It's what goes into the preparation that counts. When you put your heart and soul into something as essential as feeding another person, that's a fundamental gift. You're giving part of yourself to someone else."

Cory glanced around to find the other two women staring at Madison with the same shocked look that Cory knew was reflected on her face.

"There you have it," Ella said softly. "She's got a heart after all."

Color crept into Madison's cheeks. "Of course I do. I just don't wear it on my sleeve the way some of you do." Her gaze caught on Ella's. "And I would never cook for a man who didn't deserve the passion I put into my food."

"Speaking of that…" Cory sat forward on the bar stool where she was perched, happy to distract herself with something other than her own issues for a few minutes. "How did it go with your big date?"

Ella concentrated for a few seconds on tracing a drop of condensation down her water glass before offering a fake smile. "Turns out Toby came to town to ask me in person..."

"Ask you to be his girlfriend?" Tessa clasped her hands together.

"To ask me to be his best man—or woman, in this case. He's getting married to his high school sweetheart. They had been corresponding while he was traveling with the agency." She blew out a harsh laugh. "While he was there with me."

"Do you know laxatives can be put into food without anyone knowing?" Madison asked without missing a beat.

Ella's brows furrowed. "Are you suggesting I poison him?"

"Just enough to have him hugging the porcelain throne for a couple of days."

"It's a good idea," Tessa agreed. "Sends the right message."

"You all are demented," Ella told them, but she said it with an authentic grin. "I appreciate demented right now. If I can't be happy like Cory with her cute baby and hot bartender, then I might as well turn myself into some sort of supervillain."

Cory drew in a breath but kept her features neutral, refusing to meet Madison's assessing stare across the kitchen. She knew the other woman wouldn't discuss the truth of Cory's situation without her permission. And there was no way Cory could tell the other women the truth. She had too much at stake.

The real truth was she felt happy. Because of Kathy's presence in the house, Jordan and Cory were playing the roles of loving couple without question. Cory liked the pretend arrangement far more than she should.

As she watched Madison demonstrate a few basic cooking techniques, from making a roux to frying an egg, and explain how to use specific kitchen appliances, Cory realized that for the first time in forever, she felt normal. It was easy to forget her entire life was a sham and simply revel in the good moments. And there were so many of those.

In the past few days, she and Jordan had fallen into a routine. The mornings started with Jordan up early to make coffee and cut up fresh fruit before Ben woke. The baby would begin to gurgle, and either Cory or Jordan brought him out from the nursery. The three of them had breakfast in the sun-drenched kitchen with the scent of the surrounding pine forest coming in through the windows Jordan liked to crack open.

Jordan's mom usually joined them about a half hour later, and Ben absolutely adored his grandmother. It made Cory's heart soften with memories of her own relationship with her grandma at the same time her gut clenched thinking about how her son would never have that special bond with her mother.

They spent time hiking in the woods or checking out antiques stores around the area or browsing the wares of local artists at the Dennison Mill shopping area. On the days Jordan went to work, Cory kept his mom company. She was quickly coming to love his mother and the way she took pleasure in every activity—whether a walk around the property or a trip to town for groceries.

Kathy was a kindred spirit of sorts. The woman never spoke badly about her late husband, but Cory definitely got the impression that Jordan's father had been a harsh taskmaster and a bullish sort of man. It was obvious that Kathy regretted the distant relationship she had with her older son, and although Jordan was kind and courteous to his mom, the emotional gap between them remained.

Cory wanted to help them grow closer, both for Ben and for Jordan's sake. Especially because she knew she'd be relying on Kathy to help Jordan with parenting once he and Cory ended their arrangement.

It was going to break his mom's heart, and Cory felt like the worst sort of heel for agreeing to the whole fake-relationship farce in the first place.

"I'm not sure you have the market cornered on supervillain," she told Ella without humor.

"Trouble in paradise?" the other woman asked,

looking confused. "I thought things were going great between you and Jordan."

"They are," Cory quickly amended. "For now, anyway. I'm sure it's just a phase."

Madison barked out a laugh.

"I should go," Cory said as emotion clogged her throat. "Kathy and I are driving over to that paint-your-own-pottery place in Claremont this afternoon. I want to get Ben's food and clothes ready before we leave."

"I'll walk out with you." Today's lesson finished, Madison gathered the measuring cups and utensils she'd brought for a sort of cooking-club show-and-tell into a canvas bag.

"No need."

"I have to get to the bar anyway." The chef wiggled her eyebrows. "We're serving eggplant lasagna for the special. The lumberjack-type guys who live around here act like they hate it, but there's a wait for a table every time it's on the menu."

"Thanks for hosting the kitchen basics lesson," Cory told Tessa. She should really be thanking her new friend for giving her a place to go for a group therapy session.

"My pleasure." Tessa nodded. "You're my first houseguests."

"The decor is very you." Madison's voice dripped with sarcasm as she glanced around at the mounted animal heads hanging from the walls.

"My uncle was a hunter." Tessa cringed. "I haven't had the heart to take them down yet. They sort of keep me company."

"Don't say that." Ella made a face. "It makes you sound kind of odd."

"She is odd," Madison muttered. "You all are."

Instead of arguing, the three of them laughed. "Hey, Pot, this is Kettle calling," Cory said over her shoulder as she reached the front door. "Face it, Chef Fancy-Pants. You're as strange as the rest of us."

The other woman snorted as she followed Cory into the early-spring sunshine. Today was almost balmy, and Cory couldn't help but compare it to the constant gray of Michigan at this time of year. Once again she appreciated the surroundings, from the blue sky overhead to the fresh evergreens scenting the air. How would her life have looked if she'd taken a different path? Would she have found her way to this sort of charming setting on her own? As a kid, she'd kept scrapbooks filled with photos cut from the travel magazines her grandmother subscribed to that displayed beautiful scenes of exotic locales and destinations closer to home.

Cory had been fascinated by every spread on the national parks and other nature escapes, so to be living in this beautiful, rustic town made her feel like she was in a dream come true.

Other than the fact that it was all based on a lie.

"You're falling for him," Madison said, bumping Cory's shoulder. "You want it to be real."

"No," Cory lied without hesitation. "I know it's temporary and not real."

"You're playing house and you like it."

"Stop being mean." Cory crossed her arms over her chest with a huff. "You're supposed to be my friend."

"Since when?"

Cory had reached her car, and she turned to face the chef. "Why do you push us away?" she demanded. "It's not as if you have people coming out of the woodwork to wax poetic about your amazing personality. You know you were on the verge of being fired, right?"

"Jordan isn't going to fire me. My food brings in customers."

"The rest of the staff can't stand you. Every one of them warned me not to work with you, that you'd suck my soul from me and serve it as a daily special." Cory squeezed her hands into tight fists. "I defended you. Maybe I was wrong."

"I don't need you to defend me." Madison's voice was a reedy line of indignation. "I don't need anyone. If everyone at Trophy Room is so bothered by my presence, maybe I'll put them out of their misery and quit." She leaned closer. "Because I don't want to be where I'm not wanted or where I have to pretend to be something I'm not. I don't lie."

Cory felt the words like a blow, but she wasn't in the mood to back down. She'd done that too many times in her life before now, and it had gotten her nowhere she wanted to be.

"You're lying right now," she said, proud her voice remained steady. "You say you don't need anyone, but that's not true. You like us, and you like that we like you, even if you won't admit it. No one serves the kind of food you do without putting their heart into it. You said so yourself. We've already determined you have a heart, one that I'd guess was treated poorly by someone."

Madison looked away, blinking rapidly.

"Maybe we can both be honest, at least with each other. Yeah, I like Jordan. I wish I didn't. It would be easier for both of us. I'm an emotional train wreck, and I need to focus on getting myself together before I worry about being in a relationship." She blew out a breath and pointed a finger at the chef. "You want people to like you for more than just your food."

"Not true," Madison argued, then shook her head. "Okay, maybe true. But it's also easier if I don't care what people think of me. Things are easier with no expectations. I have a tendency to hurt people who care about me."

"You don't have to," Cory told her gently.

"You don't have to work out your relationship issues with Jordan."

Cory laughed at the shocking truth of the words. "That's a good point."

"You're too nice," Madison muttered.

"Probably," Cory admitted. "But I'm learning to like myself. And this is just the start of who I'm going to be."

The satisfying sound of logs splitting broke the quiet silence of the morning. A cold front had moved in a day earlier, bringing frigid temperatures and a layer of frost across the ground. Still, sweat dripped between Jordan's shoulder blades as he swung the ax in a familiar rhythm.

The hills around Starlight stayed cool enough most nights that he could have a fire well into late spring, but at this rate he'd have enough firewood to last a couple of years.

Physical exertion seemed like the only thing that calmed him. There weren't many moments when he missed his time on the gridiron, but this was one of them. He would have liked a productive outlet for the frustration and confusion pounding through him.

Frustration at sleeping next to Cory every night, her heat and her scent tangling in his brain and body until his fingers itched to reach for her. He stayed on his side of the bed, of course, because she was doing him a favor by pretending to be in love with him while his mom visited.

It had seemed like such a good idea to bring her to

his father's funeral as his date, a simple way to take the attention off himself and the feelings he should be able to muster about losing a parent. Feelings he couldn't access.

Nothing about Cory was simple, especially the way she made him want things he'd never dreamed of for himself. How could Jordan ever expect to be a decent father when he'd had such a poor example of one?

He remained constantly terrified of doing the wrong thing with Ben. The boy was just a baby, yet there were already so many ways Jordan could hurt him. He wondered if his mom had picked up on how much Jordan tried to avoid holding his son. It was easy to do with Grandma staying with them. His mother loved cuddling her grandson, and Jordan couldn't help but wonder why he had no memories of her showing that kind of affection with him or his brother when they were younger.

He turned to grab another log. As if he'd conjured her with his tumultuous thoughts, his mother came around the side of the house. Cory had taken Ben to town, and Jordan thought his mom had gone with them.

"That's a big pile of wood," she said, frowning at the huge stack.

"I like a fire," he said with a shrug.

"You like to burn off energy with physical activity," his mom countered, her features softening.

"I can remember you in the backyard flipping tires until well past dark most nights. You never stopped moving."

"It's what Dad expected."

Jordan cursed himself when his mom's posture went stiff. They'd had a good visit, easy and fun. He didn't want to bring up the past or memories that were difficult for both of them.

"He expected too much of you." His mom drew closer. "He pushed you too hard, but you never complained. I used to watch the two of you out the kitchen window, and I was in awe of your ability to stay strong under his coaching style."

"What choice did I have?" Jordan lowered the ax to his side as he remembered how badly his body hurt back then. Constant aches and undiagnosed injuries, which were typically unheard-of for a kid his age. "He wanted me to be perfect. You both did."

"I wanted you to be happy," Kathy said softly. "I did a bad job of letting you know it." She held out a hand. "Show me how to chop wood."

Jordan raised a brow at his fine-boned mother. "I'm not sure that's a great idea."

"Do you think you were the only one who felt like they had to be strong back then?" She leaned in and took the ax from his hand. "Oh, this is heavier than it looks."

"Mom, you're going to hurt yourself."

"No, Jordan." She leveled him with a steely stare.

"I'm healing myself and becoming stronger, things I should have started a long time ago. Something I should have managed for you and your brother."

"Did Dad hit you?" Jordan blurted, then immediately regretted the question.

His mother's eyes widened. Jordan had always wished he'd inherited her gentle eyes instead of his father's piercing green ones.

"Not after you were born," she said, almost sadly. "We got in a few knock-down, drag-out fights the first year of our marriage. I knew it would end badly for me if I kept pushing him, so I stopped. And after you were born, things seemed to get better. He was so happy to have a son, and then another when Max came along. I became like window dressing. I didn't matter to him."

"That's not true," Jordan argued. "He cared about you."

"He needed me to play a role, but you were going to be his crowning achievement."

"What a disappointment to him." Jordan laughed without humor.

"I'm not sure he would have ever been satisfied," she said instead of contradicting him. "But I knew he wasn't just pushing you. He was pushing you away. It's the biggest regret of my life that I didn't stop him."

"I allowed it to happen," Jordan told her. "Even when I was old enough to know better." He sighed.

"Even though I saw the toll it was taking on the rest of the family. We weren't really a family."

His mother blinked rapidly as she looked down at the ax, the vivid pink of her nail polish particularly bright against the worn wood of the handle. "I want to chop something."

Jordan felt a smile tug the corner of his mouth. Maybe he wasn't so unlike his mom after all.

He placed a piece of wood on the full round, showed her how to hold the ax with two hands and swing it over her head. The first time she missed the mark completely and the ax stuck in the base. But the grin she gave him made her look ten years younger, and he remembered the times he'd seen her smile like that when he was a kid. All those times involved him or his brother and their happiness.

After a few more tries, she split the log down the middle and let out a loud whoop of delight.

"You're a regular Paul Bunyan," he told her and was rewarded with her deep belly laugh.

She handed the tool back to him. "Thanks. I've got that out of my system. I see why it's so satisfying for you."

"Satisfying," he repeated, turning the word over in his head. He wasn't sure he would recognize fulfillment. He'd been trained to keep reaching, striving for more. Even after leaving football, those early lessons had continued to hold sway in his life.

He'd turned his attention toward the bar and making it into something better. But he hadn't thought about taking satisfaction from the work. He just needed to keep moving and stay busy.

"You're a good father," his mom said as they walked back to the house.

He snorted. "You've been here for less than a week. You can't possibly know that. What if…?" He pressed his lips together.

"Your dad had a lot of demons." His mother placed a hand on his arm. "He was private, and there's no point rehashing his unhappy childhood and how it manifested into the type of dad he became to you and your brother. But I see the way you look at Ben. I see how careful you are with him, Jordan. Too careful sometimes, like you can't be trusted."

"How can I be anything else?"

"Cory trusts you. She chose you, and that means something."

Those words burned in his gut. Cory hadn't chosen him. She'd chosen to walk away the morning after they were together. Even now, he didn't know how much she wanted from him, and it scared the hell out of him how much he wanted from her. Jordan liked hard work and he was fine with giving maximum effort, but he wanted control. There had been too many years when he hadn't been in charge of any aspect of his life. Unfortunately, he'd never felt more out of control than he had since Cory and Ben showed up in his life.

But he couldn't tell his mom any of that. They'd mended a piece of their relationship in her time here. He wouldn't take the chance on ripping that apart so soon.

"I want to do the right thing by my boy," he said, because that was the truth.

"Then that's what you'll do," his mom said, and the unwavering faith in her tone made his throat sting.

He hoped he could be the man to deserve that faith.

Chapter Thirteen

"Don't look now, but the boss is coming this way, and he looks mad as a cat in the bath."

Cory glanced up from where she was stirring a marinara sauce to see Jordan moving toward her.

"Did I just say don't look?" Madison nudged her hip as she walked by.

"Everyone looks when someone says 'don't look.'"

"Another example of why I stay away from people," the chef told her, then waved to Jordan. "Hey, there. What brings you to my fair section of this fine establishment?" She threw up her hands when Jordan frowned at her like she'd just kicked him in the shin. "Come on, Jordan. Don't tell me you've had more complaints about my attitude. I've been flippin' sunshine and roses lately."

Cory hid her grin as Madison turned toward the line cook and servers gathering plates of food. "Tell him my mood is set to unicorns pooping rainbows all the time now."

"A hundred percent unicorn poop," Misty said with a cheeky grin.

"I appreciate the effort," Jordan told Madison. "You even got mentioned in a Yelp review yesterday."

Her eyes narrowed. "What did they say?"

"That the quality of the food was enhanced by how professional and lovely the chef was when she came out of the kitchen to personally greet them."

"Professional and lovely. Exactly." Madison nodded. "I remember that sniveling couple. The husband had some hang-up about how none of his food could touch, so we had to serve everything in individual bowls. Pain in my—"

"Unicorns," Cory reminded her friend, then felt joy flutter through her. She really did consider Madison a friend. Misty, Tanya and the other Trophy Room employees, too. Ella Samuelson was watching Ben tonight since Kathy had left yesterday. Cory would miss Jordan's mom, especially since she wasn't sure when or if she'd have a chance to see the other woman again.

"Can I talk to you for a minute?" Jordan crooked a finger at her. "Out back."

"Kind of busy," Cory said with a wooden smile. She absolutely did not want to speak with Jordan. She wasn't sure if he noticed that she'd been avoiding him without his mom in the house to act as a buffer. By the look on his face, he had.

"It's fine." Madison grabbed the wooden spoon from her hand. "Take all the time you need."

Cory shot her a death glare, which Madison responded to with a wide grin. "Unicorns," she said in a singsong voice.

"Thanks," Cory muttered, then glanced at Jordan. "I need to wash my hands."

"I'll wait."

Heat crept into Cory's cheeks as she felt the rest of the kitchen staff watching her. She washed her hands under the big industrial faucet, then dried them with a paper towel, careful to make her movements measured and not like she was nervous or dreading whatever conversation Jordan wanted to have.

He didn't talk or joke with his employees the way she'd become used to. One of things she appreciated most about the way Jordan ran his business was that he remembered personal details about each person who worked for him. Birthdays, anniversaries or even when someone's dog had been to the vet. But now he stood in stony silence, and Cory couldn't help but feel like she was being called to the proverbial principal's office.

She followed him through the kitchen to the hallway door that led to the alley behind the bar.

"You're embarrassing me," she told him as the door shut behind her. He inclined his head but didn't respond other than a slight hardening of his gaze. Cory rubbed her hands against her arms to ward off the evening chill. After the scents and sounds of the busy kitchen, the quiet of the dark night felt almost ominous. "Seriously, everyone is going to think we're in some huge fight or came out here for a quickie. Either way, it makes me look bad. You're the boss, and I'm your fiancée."

"You're not my fiancée," he said, his voice a low growl. "If you were, I wouldn't pull you into a dank alley for a quickie."

She blew out a breath. "You know what I mean."

"Actually, I do." He ran a hand through his hair. "Parker stopped in tonight on his way to pick up Anna from gymnastics class. He heard from one of the Realtors in town that you were looking at apartments on the other side of Starlight yesterday afternoon. He wanted to make sure we were doing okay."

"Oh." Cory cringed. "I wanted to give you some time with your mom before she left, and I thought it would be good to have a plan for when…" She waved a hand in the air. "The breakup."

"Do you think that's something we should have discussed?"

Cory didn't know how to discuss the end of this pretend relationship without making a fool of herself. She didn't want it to end—heck, she dreaded moving her things out of his bedroom—but wasn't about to admit that to Jordan. She couldn't stand the potential of seeing pity in his eyes.

She'd left the house, hoping Jordan and his mom would talk before Kathy left. The pain on the other woman's face was clear each time she looked at her son. She desperately wanted to be closer to Jordan, and although he wouldn't discuss it, Cory knew he wanted the same thing.

Her intention hadn't been to look for a new place to live, but when she'd passed the two-story brick house with a For Rent sign in the yard, she'd called. She'd hoped that looking for a place to call her own would help ease the ache that came every time she thought about leaving Jordan's home. The cabin in the woods felt like her home, as well, and that would only add to her heartbreak when her arrangement with Jordan ended.

"I'm sorry," she said simply. "I don't know how to make any of this okay. We barged into your life and turned it upside down."

She dashed a hand over her cheek when a tear escaped. Damn, she didn't want to cry right now. "I know you were doing fine before this, Jordan. You have a home and a business. I've already come to love Starlight…"

She swallowed when the words *and you* almost fell from her mouth. Admitting her feelings for this man would lead to nothing but agony. She didn't want to scare him off when she wanted so badly for him to be a part of Ben's life. Their son was the most important part of their relationship. "It's obvious you don't want us at the house, and I—"

"What do you mean, I don't want you there?" He took a step closer to her, and longing skittered across her nerve endings. "Hell, Cory. I painted a damn nursery for the baby. I can barely keep my hands off you at night. Do you know how little I was sleeping with you next to me?"

"You never want to hold him," she whispered, pain slicing through her heart. The small rejection of her son felt like a rejection to her, as well.

Jordan's gaze shuttered, and he glanced away.

"It's okay," she said quickly, because letting people off easily was her way. "I know you never expected to be a father. I'm hoping that as he gets older and can do more, you'll want to be a part of his life. Ben deserves to have two parents that love him."

"Of course he does. I want to be a part of his life. He's my son. I just don't want to screw him up the way my dad did me and my brother."

"You're not going to," she told him. "You're a good man and you'll be a great father."

"Did you and my mom get together and rehearse what you were going to say to me?" he asked, then laughed softly.

"I didn't talk to your mom about this. I haven't talked to anyone."

He reached out and linked their fingers together. "Talk to me."

Oh, if only it were that easy. "You know I was raised by a single mom. When I got old enough to ask about my dad, she told me he left when I was a baby because it was too much trouble to be a parent."

She forced a steady breath. "I took that to mean I was too much trouble. I don't want you to leave. Or in this case, to tell us to leave. I like it here, Jordan. We don't have to be a couple to raise our son together. But I'm trying not to put pressure on you for more than you can give."

"You're not."

"Why don't you want to be a dad?" she asked.

He started to release his grip on her, but Cory held on. No way was she going to let him go at this moment. "It's not that I don't want to. I don't know how. You're a natural, and I feel like a bull in a china shop trying to take care of a baby."

"You stayed with him and you both survived."

He sighed, and there was so much emotion packed into that breath. "I want Ben to do more than survive. Surviving is the easy part. He's my son. I want him to thrive."

"We'll make sure he does," Cory said. She pulled him closer and wrapped her arms around his waist. In the intimacy of the dark alley, it seemed easier to let down her guard. Her rational mind might know it was better to keep her distance, but she put those thoughts aside for a moment.

His heartbeat was a steady rhythm as she rested her head against his chest. Once again, he cradled it like she was precious to him. Oh, how she wanted to be precious to this strong, steady man. Even if it ended with her heart in tatters.

They stopped serving food at the bar at ten, so Cory had made it home several hours earlier than Jordan the previous night. He'd returned in the wee hours to a quiet house, a big part of him hoping that Cory would be waiting in his bed.

He shouldn't want her there. He should know enough to keep his distance. Yet even though each night of his mom's visit had been torture to lie in bed next to Cory without touching her, even that tiny bit of closeness was something he'd come to crave.

His bed had been empty, and his heart ached at the realization their days together in this house would quickly come to an end. Hell, did he need another sign besides her looking for rental properties?

She'd gone along with the pretend relationship because he'd asked her to, but it wasn't what she wanted. He wasn't what she wanted.

He'd crawled into bed and fallen into a restless sleep, catching faint whiffs of her perfume clinging to the sheets as he tossed and turned. Even his bedding didn't want to give her up.

As soon as the first rays of light filtered through his blinds, he'd gotten up and started the coffee. He had to be back at Trophy Room for a late-morning meeting with Brynn to discuss the upcoming Maker's Market weekend at the Dennison Mill. He was making the bar an integral piece of the community. More than just a local watering hole. He wanted his establishment to mean something to the people of Starlight.

Jordan was on his second cup of coffee when he heard Ben babbling from the nursery. The boy usually woke from his nap grumpy, but mornings were the baby's happiest time. He greeted each day with a gummy grin and feet pumping. One of Jordan's favorite moments each day had quickly become when Cory—or his mom—brought Ben to the kitchen. The baby would grin and reach for him, effectively melting Jordan's heart.

But his mom was gone, and the babbling continued with no other sound. Was Cory testing him? Had his admission about his fear of being a father made her want him to prove his mettle?

It was silly. His nerves were silly. As she'd pointed out to him, Jordan had stayed with Ben on his own. He'd managed it a few times now. He'd changed diapers and only once put the baby's pants on backward. Not a huge mistake in the grand scheme of things.

He could handle the morning if she needed him to. He would have to handle it, because Cory wouldn't be with him forever.

The ache in his chest as he thought about that on the way to the nursery had him drawing a slow breath. He opened the door and flipped on the light.

"Good morning, bud," he said as he approached the crib.

Ben was on his back, holding his pajama-clad feet and rocking from one side to the other like some sort of miniature yogi. He threw his hands over his head when he spotted Jordan.

Okay, that was a good start.

Now he just needed to deal with the rest.

As Jordan picked up the baby, Ben darted a glance around the room. "Mommy is sleeping in today," Jordan told the boy, although secretly he wondered if Cory was listening to his conversation with their son through the baby monitor.

Great. He could add paranoid along with terrified to his list of go-to emotions for fatherhood.

"Let's start with a clean diaper." He flipped off the monitor, then put Ben on the changing pad.

"I can do that," a rough voice said behind him.

He looked over his shoulder, almost surprised to find Cory standing in the doorway. Or propped against the doorway, was more like it.

"Are you okay?" he asked as she pressed the heel of her hand to her forehead. "Big night once you got off work?"

Jordan knew the younger members of his staff sometimes partied together at the end of their shift. The thought that Cory had joined them shouldn't bother him.

He respected her right to make whatever decisions about her life she wanted.

But he wanted to be a factor in that process almost more than he wanted his next breath.

"Head cold," she muttered, then took an unsteady step forward. "I could feel it starting with a throat tickle yesterday, so I took some zinc and vitamins. They didn't work."

"Don't take this the wrong way, but you look like hell."

"I feel worse," she admitted, then coughed into her elbow.

"Go back to bed."

"I need to take care of Ben." She tried for a smile, but it looked more like a grimace. "Moms don't get the day off. It's not that kind of job."

"It is when the dad can pitch in."

"You have things to do." She coughed again. "Important things."

"I'm doing the most important thing right now." He turned to Ben. "Tell her we've got this."

The boy cooed in response, earning a soft chuckle from Cory.

"You sound like a two-pack-a-day bourbon drinker," Jordan told her. "Go to bed, Cory. I'll wake you if we need anything."

"Okay." She came forward and grinned down at Ben. "Mommy's not going to get too close because she wants you to stay well. Take it easy on your daddy, sweetheart. I'll see you soon." She placed a hand on Jordan's arm. "Thank you. I'm glad he has you. I'm glad we both do."

"Sure," Jordan said. If only he felt confident telling her how much of him she truly had. "I'll put a glass of water and a bottle of cold medicine on your nightstand once I get him changed. If there's anything else you need, let me know."

"Thank you." She backed up, sneezed into her elbow, then disappeared out the door.

Jordan felt her absence like an itch he couldn't reach but reminded himself he wasn't truly alone. If something happened, Cory was available. And it was a morning. He could manage on his own.

After dressing Ben and delivering the supplies to Cory's nightstand, he fed the baby breakfast and then checked the time. He felt a bit foolish toting the baby along to a business meeting. Not because he didn't want to have Ben with him, but he worried that it would be clear to everyone how out of his league Jordan was as a father.

He was used to succeeding. He liked that people in town knew him as someone in control of his life.

Clearly a baby would change all of that. He just wondered how much of a change he'd be in for today.

Turned out Jordan's fears were unfounded. Ben was more enticing than an adorable puppy or free rein in a candy store.

Jordan had shown up to the meeting with Ben harnessed to his chest. The baby seemed to like the carrier. Although Jordan's first instinct was to apologize for bringing his son along, he didn't have a chance to speak before the other business owners descended on him like a swarm of oohing and aahing locusts.

Several of the women—Brynn and Kaitlin in particular—offered to hold Ben, but to Jordan's great surprise, the baby fussed each time someone reached for him. Ben buried his face into Jordan's shoulder and held on for dear life. The sense of accomplishment Jordan took from that was ridiculous, but he couldn't seem to stop it.

He didn't want to stop it.

As the meeting progressed, he took Ben out of the carrier, bounced the boy on his knee, walked around the room with him and generally multitasked in a way that would have seemed impossible just a few short weeks ago.

Jordan felt like a real parent. The kind he never could have imagined becoming.

Once things wrapped up, he started to strap Ben back into his front pack when the most god-awful noise came from the boy, followed quickly by an equally god-awful smell.

Jordan realized he'd made the rookiest of all rookie mistakes. He'd left the diaper bag at home. Such a small issue in some respects, but it seemed to represent everything he doubted about his ability to handle fatherhood.

His palms started to sweat as Ben fussed and squirmed. "Little buddy, I'm going to get you home as soon as possible."

Although if he drove a maximum of five miles over the speed limit, it would take twenty minutes to reach his house. Long enough for that mess to be hardened and caked onto the baby's soft bottom, with Ben crying the entire way.

Oh, he was a terrible dad.

"You're a natural," Josh said as Jordan walked by where the other man stood with Brynn. They were looking at something on her laptop, situated on the table in front of them.

"I'm the opposite of that," Jordan muttered. "I forgot the damn diaper bag, and Ben needs a change in the worst way."

"I've got extra in my car." Brynn pushed back from the table. "Ben looks like he's around the same size as my daughter, Remi. They might not be the perfect fit, but better than a stinky bottom."

"Extra," Jordan repeated. "Is that a thing parents do? Keep extra supplies on hand for emergencies?"

Brynn glanced at Josh, who shrugged. "It's mainly moms who take care of that kind of stuff, although as a single dad, I learned to become equipped for emergencies."

"I need to get equipped." Jordan smoothed a hand over Ben's downy hair. "But I'll gladly take a diaper from you. Next round of wings is on the house in return."

"That's a great trade," Brynn said with a grin. For being a tiny woman, she could put away wings like nobody's business.

She closed the laptop and dropped it into her tote bag. He followed her and Josh out of the meeting room.

"I'd be happy to bring over some chicken soup for Cory," Brynn offered. "Ella says great things about her. Finn and his dad were worried when Ella left her traveling nurse agency so suddenly to return to Starlight. She didn't seem interested in making friends. But it seems like she's already gotten close with Cory and the other two women in their little cooking club."

Josh nodded. "Your scary chef has a kinder, gentler side. Cory has brought it out."

"Apparently," Jordan agreed, although inside he chided himself for not asking more about Cory's new friends. "Cory texted me at the start of the meeting.

She said the extra sleep helped her feel better. I'll let you know about the soup."

Brynn opened the back door of her car and handed Jordan a fresh diaper and a small package of wipes. "I like extra ranch with my wings," she said, winking.

He nodded. "Done."

"You and Cory should come to our weekly friends' dinner this weekend."

"Yeah, maybe." Jordan took a step back. "Josh invited us last week, but my mom was in town."

"Well, I'm not just inviting. I'm insisting."

"Listen to her," Josh advised. "Brynn tends to get what she wants. She talks soft and carries a big stick."

"Good to know." Jordan held up the diaper. "I'm going to go take care of business."

"See you later, then." Brynn climbed into her car as Jordan turned away.

"Hey, barman." Josh grinned. "You're not alone in this parenting thing. You know that, right?"

"You gonna change this diaper?"

"That's not what I'm talking about, and hell, no. But I'm here for you. All the guys are here for you."

"Thanks." Jordan cleared his throat. "I appreciate it."

Unfortunately, he'd never felt more alone in his life.

Chapter Fourteen

The following week, Cory lifted on her toes to return a serving bowl to a high cabinet in Jordan's kitchen.

"You don't have to do that," Jordan said as he walked into the kitchen. "I told you I'd empty the dishwasher once Ben went down for his nap."

"I had a cold, and it's gone now," she reminded him. "I'm totally healthy and able to pitch in again."

"I know," he said, coming to stand behind her and taking the bowl from her fingers. At his height, he barely had to stretch to place it on the top shelf. "I like taking care of you and Ben."

Cory felt the breath whoosh out of her lungs at his comment. Or maybe it was the heat of his body so close to hers. She would have liked to blame the moment on a sudden recurrence of the fever that had plagued her the first twenty-four hours of her illness. Delusional would be a good excuse, not to mention a perfect description for her reaction to Jordan.

"As much as I appreciate it, that's not your job." She forced herself to move away from him. "I've been taking care of myself for a lot of years."

She grabbed the utensil holder from the dishwasher rack and busied herself with putting more items away. Anything so she didn't have to look directly at Jordan. Not when she feared she wouldn't be able to hide her emotions.

Since she'd woken last week feeling like someone had taken a sledgehammer to her head, she'd seen a different side of him. Cory didn't know if he'd really lost his fear about being a father or was stepping into the role because she needed him, but either way, he was doing a darn good job of making her fall even harder for him than she had been before.

He'd taken off work so that Ella wouldn't have to come by and had single-handedly parented Ben while simultaneously playing nurse to Cory. She hated being sick and feeling weak and helpless. She'd spent too long feeling helpless.

"You don't have to do everything on your own," he reminded her. "You're not alone."

But she was. In some ways she always had been. Growing up with a single mom who resented her daughter and while in a relationship with a man who saw her as nothing more than an extension of himself. She'd surrounded herself with people who didn't care about her the way they should. It left her feeling as alone as if she were in solitary confinement. In some ways, that was how she felt most comfortable.

Jordan made her question everything. His low-key way of caring made her want to release her defenses and her habit of isolating herself emotionally. It had been a means to self-preservation, but now it just felt like she was being a coward.

"We should come up with a plan for ending this." A spoon slipped from her fingers as she said the words, clattering to the floor and grating against her already worn nerves.

She and Jordan bent to pick it up at the same time.

"Why?" he asked softly. "We've got a good thing going here, Cory."

"It's not real." She quickly grabbed the utensil before he could.

He didn't respond to those three words, and she hated that she wanted him to. She wanted him to tell her it was real. Or it could be. Because being here at this house with him felt like every dream of a perfect life she'd ever imagined coming true.

"I'll do whatever you want," he said quietly.

Did she hear disappointment in his tone?

She blinked against the sudden rush of tears to her eyes. Wasn't that just the problem? She couldn't tell him what she wanted, because that might make her seem weak. But she didn't have the strength to risk her heart again.

"We can give it a few more days," she offered, unsure of how to navigate this minefield of emotions.

Jordan nodded. "If you're really doing okay, I'm going to head into the bar for a few hours. I need to get caught up on some things and work out the staff for the beer tent at the Maker's Market."

"Sure," she agreed as she felt the distance between them grow. It was a distance she should cling to, but she hated it. "I'm really feeling much better. Thank you for everything, Jordan. I promise you don't have to take care of me."

Tell me again that you like it, she thought, but he didn't say anything. Just turned and grabbed his keys from the counter, then headed out the door.

She spent the rest of the day wishing she'd handled that conversation better. Ben woke after his nap, and she strapped him into his carrier and took him for a walk on the trails that bordered the property.

The clean scent of pine and the crunch of old leaves beneath her feet seemed to relax her enough that she was able to draw a deep breath and think about her situation in a more rational way. It was difficult to keep her wits about her around Jordan, when everything about him made her want to lose herself.

She couldn't lose herself again. Not when she was on the verge of truly finding who she was. The time had come to decide who she wanted to be and go after it.

Jordan texted late in the afternoon to tell her the bar was slammed. He'd sent Tanya home with the start of a similar cold to Cory's.

U okay?

That simple question gutted Cory, because despite how they'd left things earlier and the tension about the future, he cared enough to ask. She could imagine how busy he was on a hectic night at the bar and everything that entailed. Being pulled in a dozen different directions. Yet she knew without a doubt he would drop everything and return to her if she gave him any indication she needed him.

She wouldn't do that.

After returning his message, she fed Ben, gave him a bath and read him stories until bedtime. With the house to herself, she pulled out the jewelry supplies she'd brought with her from Michigan and began to craft a series of gemstone earrings using the labradorite chips she'd bought from a thrift store in her hometown.

The way the women she'd met in town seemed to love the earrings and necklaces she wore reminded her how much she'd loved the art of making jewelry. She'd picked up the hobby in high school and even sold some of her pieces at a local gift shop during college but hadn't seemed to find time for the practice when she moved to Atlanta. It was nice to have the space to finally think about who she wanted to be. To finally get to the place where she could figure out who she was because she didn't have to be anything else.

But the one thing she wanted to be—with Jordan in truth—was something she couldn't have the way things stood between them now. She hadn't earned her happy ending with a man like him, but the more time she spent with him, the more she wanted to try.

It was nearly two in the morning when Jordan let himself into the quiet house. Cory had left the copper fixture on over the sink, so he didn't bother to flip on any other lights as he moved toward his bedroom.

She did that every time he closed the bar, and he'd quickly gotten used to taking the last turn on his winding driveway to see the glow beckoning to him from the front window. It made his house feel like a home in a way that shocked him for such a small change.

But it was more than the light, he knew. It was the feeling that someone was waiting for him. Someone cared about his return. He wasn't alone.

He'd thought he'd liked living alone until Cory and Ben. Now he realized he'd just gotten used to the solitude because it was easier than anything else.

He'd never thought of himself as someone who took the easy path, but he'd done that in his emotional life.

As had become his habit, he cracked open the door of the nursery and spent a few minutes watching Ben sleep. The bar had been host to two bachelorette parties plus one reunion of high school friends, and Jordan hadn't stopped moving, pouring drinks or talking to customers since the moment he walked in.

He didn't realize how keyed up he was until the stillness in his son's room eased the tension that filled him. He wanted to slip into Cory's room the same way, but he was afraid that might make him an inappropriate creeper.

He'd just taken off his watch and set it on the tall dresser in the master bedroom when a sound caught his attention.

Cory lay asleep on his bed, on top of the covers, as if she'd dozed off there without meaning to.

Every nerve ending in Jordan's body went on high alert. It was like his fantasy life had thrown a party, and this was his dream come true. Like most dreams, once achieved, he wanted more. Suddenly it wasn't enough to watch her. He wanted to hold her in his arms, to bury his face in her hair and breathe in the citrusy fragrance that always clung to her.

He wanted so much more.

Not a creeper, he reminded himself. He wasn't sure what had led her into his room, but he had a feeling she could easily be scared off again. He still couldn't believe how much his feelings had changed in the past couple of weeks. He tried and failed to access any of the initial anger he'd felt when she'd shown up in his life with a baby he hadn't known about. Maybe the anger could protect him.

He still wished that she would have told him about Ben earlier, but Jordan understood she hadn't been in the best place emotionally. He also took responsibility for the way he'd left Atlanta without speaking to her.

Walking away and changing his number had seemed like the simplest course of action if she'd gone back to Kade. If he'd stayed, he would have spent months waiting and hoping for her to call. Too much time devoted to wondering if he should reach out to her.

But he hadn't known what would result from their night together.

Now he did. What was the saying?

When you know better, you do better.

He had to do better for both of them.

He stripped off his clothes and put on a fresh T-shirt and shorts. No way was he going to wake her smelling like stale beer.

Hell, he wished he didn't have to wake her at all.

Maybe the right thing to do—the better thing—would be to retreat to the couch for the night and leave her in peace.

He wasn't quite that much of a better man.

The mattress sagged with his weight as he sat on the edge of it. Cory's skin felt like silk as he gently shook her arm.

"Sweetheart, wake up."

She mumbled something incoherent, then shifted and snuggled against his pillow. He felt a smile tug the corner of his mouth. Cory didn't wake easy and sunny like Ben.

Okay, he'd tried. Maybe not the most valiant effort, but he'd made some attempt.

He moved to the other side of the bed and pulled back the sheet and comforter. His hands fisted as he resisted the urge to draw Cory closer, his own personal soothing blanket. She made him feel secure in a way he hadn't realized was lacking from his life. Like she was some sort of lighthouse in the storm of whatever might come his way, a true north that would always guide him home.

Except there was no always between them. There was just a temporary arrangement that she seemed more than ready to end.

He never wanted it to end.

With a deep breath, Jordan closed his eyes and willed his body to relax. A moment later he heard a startled gasp and turned his head to find Cory staring at him in the faint light of moon glow that came from his bedroom window.

"I tried to wake you," he said immediately.

She didn't answer for a moment, then said softly, "I like your bed."

Her voice was sleep-rough, her eyes heavy, and it was all he could do not to groan in response.

"Then stay," he managed and did his best to gather all his gentlemanly instincts. "I can move to the couch if you want."

"I want you to stay," she answered without hesitation.

Then, as if every one of his dreams was coming true, she leaned forward and pressed her mouth to his.

Jordan's body went into overdrive, but he tamped down the need to move too quickly. He let her set the pace. This was a gift, and he was smart enough to cherish it.

His measured response must have been the right one. Cory shifted closer, her small frame pressed against the length of him. He inwardly cursed the layers of bedding that separated them.

"How was your night?" she asked between kisses.

"This is the best part of it." He threaded his fingers in her hair, reveling in the feel of the soft strands.

She moved again, lifting herself to straddle his hips as she balanced her weight on her hands on either side of his head. Her hair fell around him like a cocoon, and he wanted to stay in this moment forever.

"Can I tell you a secret?"

"Yeah, sweetheart. You can tell me anything."

"I was dreaming about you before I woke up."

"The kind of dream where you're naked and in front of a crowd of people?" he asked with a smile.

She shook her head, the ends of her hair tickling his neck. "The kind of dream where you and I are alone and we're both naked."

"I like your version better," he said, not bothering to keep the desire from his tone. He was so damn tired of hiding how much he wanted her. For all he knew, she was sleep seducing him, but he'd take whatever she was willing to give him.

"Me too." She sat up and tugged the pajama shirt over her head.

To his eternal gratitude, she wasn't wearing a bra.

He lifted his hands and drew his thumbs over the tight peaks of her nipples before holding the weight of her breasts.

She moaned low in her throat and leaned forward to kiss him again, but he shifted her forward so he could take her breast into his mouth. He gave attention to one and then the other, savoring the sweet and salty taste of her.

Then she leaned down to kiss him again, deep and long. He lifted her up and off him so he could pull down the covers. He needed to be closer to her, to feel her skin against his. To be inside her.

But maybe he should have turned on the night-stand light, because suddenly they were tangled in covers, arms flailing and legs kicking as they tried to get to each other.

Cory's laughter rang out in the dark room. "I'm stuck in the sheet."

"Damn sheet," he muttered and turned his attention to freeing her.

She laughed again, and the sound made Jordan's heart feel like it was filled with champagne bubbles, light and fizzy. He'd never thought of sex as fizzy. He was the down-and-dirty type. As with everything else, Cory helped him see a new perspective that made something already awesome even better.

They were both breathing hard and laughing just as hard by the time he untangled her and threw back the covers. She flopped on the mattress next to him. "Wow, that was a bit of a mood dampener, huh?"

"Not one bit." He took her hand and brought it to his mouth, kissing each of her knuckles. "I can't imagine anything that would dampen my desire for you."

She squeezed his hand. "Then you'd best get naked, my friend. Because I've got some dreams, and you're just the man to make them come true."

With that kind of a command, how could he do anything but follow it? Minutes—or hours—later, he sheathed himself in a condom and slid inside her. The sigh she let out was like music to his ears, and it felt like coming home.

They moved together, all thought of laughter put

aside for the moment. As good as it had been with Cory before, something was different this time. Jordan wanted more, and he got it. Their connection seemed deeper, and he couldn't imagine how or why they would end their arrangement in any way but making it real.

If she needed time to get used to the idea, he'd give that to her. If she needed space, it was hers. But whether or not she wanted to talk about it now or pretend otherwise, they belonged to each other.

Of that he had no doubt.

And when they went over the edge of desire together, holding each other tight, it was as if the universe was giving him a sign of how right this was. They were meant to be.

As he held her close while their breathing went back to normal, she smiled against his mouth. "That was better than any dream I ever had."

Filled with hope and an overwhelming sense of peace, he couldn't agree more.

Chapter Fifteen

Sunday evening, Jordan parked the car on the street in front of Nick Dunlap's Craftsman bungalow. "You don't have to be nervous."

"I'm not nervous," Cory lied.

"They're nice people."

"Of course you think that. They're your friends."

She closed her eyes and tried to steady her breath, knowing she was being ridiculous but unable to stop herself. When Jordan had suggested attending the Sunday supper party at Nick and Brynn's house, it had seemed like a great idea. Mara and Parker would be there, along with her daughter, Evie. Josh and his daughter, Evie's best friend, Anna, were coming, as well.

"Actually, they're not really my friends."

She glanced toward Jordan. "What do you mean?"

"I mean, they're my customers. They come into the bar on a regular basis for a drink and a meal. I like all of them, and they seem like the kind of people who would make good friends. But I don't have friends. I have coworkers and customers."

"That's not true," she argued. "Josh gave up an entire morning to help you redo the nursery."

"And I'm comping his employees a happy-hour game night at the bar."

"Everyone in town likes you, Jordan. At least everyone I've talked to."

"I'm the local bartender," he told her with a laugh. "I pour beer. Who doesn't like the guy who pours beer?" He took her hand. "This is new for me, Cory. I'm not much for socializing. It's out of my comfort zone. Hell, don't forget how we met. Most of the team was inside whooping it up at the party, and I was sitting alone on the side of your pool."

"I'm glad you were there," she said softly, running a thumb over a scar on his pointer finger. "And that you're here. I'm glad we're doing this together, even if it's hard for me to open up to these people."

He frowned. "Everyone who meets you loves you. You already have a foursome of friends, and you're thick as thieves, from what I can tell."

She shrugged. "Those women are like me, not quite broken but definitely a little banged up and bent in places. The people in that house have their lives together. I feel like they're going to take one look at me and know I don't belong. That everything between us is fake."

"Not everything. At least I don't think you could have faked me making all those dreams come true last night."

"I'll give you that," she said, feeling a blush creep up her cheeks at the memory of how many times he'd made her dreams come true.

"You gave me a lot more." He leaned in and brushed a kiss across her temple.

Ben let out a happy shriek from the back seat, making Cory grin. Was it possible a baby could pick up on the connection between his parents? She'd noticed that Ben seemed to express his happiness every time he saw his parents touch.

"We should go in." She looked toward the house again. "I just hope these people don't turn on me if I'm no longer a part of your life."

"We have a son together, Cory. We'll always be a part of each other's lives."

She nodded and got out of the car, unwilling to let Jordan see how much the thought affected her. Of course, they'd always have a part in each other's lives. But the idea of Ben being the only thing that held them together hurt her heart. She didn't want to believe that. There was no way to believe it when the truth was so much more for her.

Cory wasn't pretending to be in love with Jordan. She'd fallen for him, and she knew how badly her heart would break when they ended this.

Nick opened the front door with a wide smile. "Good to see you out from behind the bar," he told Jordan with an enthusiastic handshake before turning to Cory. "I hear we have your better half to thank for the change in everyone's favorite solitary bar owner."

"I'm Cory," she said, offering her hand. "It's nice to meet you."

"The pleasure is all mine."

Jordan held up a couple of the growlers of beer he'd picked up from the bar on their way over. "You can take a bartender out into the real world, but lucky for you, I travel with beer."

"Thanks, man." Nick led them into the house, and Cory followed, trying to tamp down the nerves that bubbled up again.

Nick seemed nice enough and not as intimidating as she would have imagined for an officer of the law, but his casual comment about Jordan being the favorite reminded her once again that she would be the outsider when their arrangement ended.

It would end because it had to. Her feelings for Jordan were already too overwhelming. They threatened to outstrip her good sense and her commitment to making herself a priority.

She pasted a smile on her face despite her tumbling emotions as Nick led them into a bright kitchen painted in a soft yellow with maple cabinets and a beautiful granite counter. She greeted Mara and Brynn and was introduced to Mara's husband, Parker. She also finally got the chance to personally thank Josh for his help with the nursery.

"The girls are in the basement playing Ping-Pong," Brynn told her as the men went into the family room to watch a basketball game. Brynn held a baby girl who looked to be near Ben's age. "This is our daughter, Remi. She's seven months now." The baby was adorable—although not nearly as big as Ben, she seemed just as happy.

Cory held her baby a little tighter. "Ben is almost seven months old, as well."

"They'll grow up together." Brynn grinned. "Best friends, I'm sure."

As much as Cory loved the thought of those kinds of lifelong friendships for her son, she could also imagine a future where she'd be alone with only Ben. What if Jordan eventually found a woman to settle down with? Someone who wasn't her. What if her son had half siblings and she had no one other than her cooking-club friends and whatever job she ended up finding once she left the bar?

"Did I say something wrong?" Brynn asked gently.

"Because you look like she just kicked your puppy," Mara added, earning an eye roll from Brynn.

"Ignore her," Brynn said.

"She works with Madison Maurer," Mara reminded her friend. "My level of snark is nowhere near hers."

The easy banter between the two helped Cory to relax the tiniest bit. "It's nothing. I just didn't exactly grow up in a tight-knit community. Sometimes the easy camaraderie of this place overwhelms me."

"Girl, same." Mara pointed to herself. "Sometimes it's overwhelming, and sometimes it's nauseating."

"It's never nauseating," Brynn argued. "But it can be a lot to handle."

Cory frowned. "Jordan said you're a Starlight native. Don't you get used to it?"

Mara and Brynn shared a look. "There are great things about small-town life," Brynn said after a moment. "But even if you grow up in it, having people know your business or thinking that they understand you better than you understand yourself is a challenge sometimes." She rested a hand on Remi's head, and the girl snuggled against her chest. "Plus, people like to judge others or what they don't understand. You have to learn to ignore it."

"I've never been great at ignoring other people's opinions."

"This is your chance to choose who matters to you. You get that choice."

Cory let out a long breath. She hadn't expected to jump right in with a deep, emotional conversation at a dinner party, but being honest and then supported for it did wonders for her confidence.

"I appreciate you connecting me with Ella," she told Mara. "She's been a lifesaver staying with Ben while I work." She glanced at Brynn. "She takes care of Remi during the day, as well, right?"

"I'd be lost without her," Brynn admitted. "Although, I kept waiting for her to tell me she's heading back to her traveling nurse career. I'm not sure anyone expected her to stay in town this long."

Cory got the same impression but didn't mention it.

"But you're here for the long haul," Mara observed, her gaze steady on Cory. "Jordan certainly did a good job of playing his cards close to the vest on the relationship front. No one had any idea about you and Ben."

Including Jordan, Cory wanted to say. Once again, she hated lying to the people in this town. She didn't know much about either of these women, but they didn't strike her as the type who'd think badly of her for how she'd handled her pregnancy and the months after Ben's birth.

"There was so much to deal with after Ben's surgery," she said, because that much wasn't a lie.

"I can't imagine what you went through or how you handled it on your own," Brynn said.

Cory shrugged and offered what she hoped was a reassuring smile. As nice as these women seemed, she didn't want to relive that time again. "He's healthy now, and I'm so grateful. We're focused on the future."

Brynn squeezed her arm. "I respect that. Speaking of the future…" She leaned in to study Cory's earrings. "Mara tells me you're a jewelry designer."

"Hardly," Cory said with a laugh. "I used to make things to wear and I sold a few pieces, but I'm just getting back into it. I took a few art classes in college, but don't have any actual expertise."

"You have talent," Mara said. "That's obvious. I'd totally wear that necklace."

"Thanks." Cory pressed a finger to the beaded chain she wore, a blush rising to her cheeks at the way the two women were studying her.

"Have you heard about the upcoming Maker's Market we're hosting at Dennison Mill?" Brynn asked. "In addition to our regular shop vendors, we're inviting other local artisans to set up booths around the property. We've done the event before, and it's been really popular. There isn't a lot of time, but if you want me to save a space for you, I'm sure our customers would love your designs."

"That's a lovely offer, but…" Cory paused and swallowed back her refusal. In truth, the idea of selling her jewelry appealed to her in a way she couldn't explain. It might be difficult to craft enough items to make it worth it, although she'd fashioned a dozen pair of earrings just the other night while Jordan was at the bar. She'd gotten so caught up in the relaxing rhythm of her work that she hadn't even realized how much she'd done or how late it was until the grand-father clock in his family room chimed midnight.

"Can I think about it and give you a call tomor-row morning?" she asked Brynn. "I'll have to take a look at my supplies and the timing to figure out if it's something I could manage."

"But you'll consider it?" Brynn grinned. "I'm so happy. Yes, call me whenever."

The guys came back into the kitchen at that mo-ment, and the rest of the evening went by in a series of bright and easy moments filled with laughter and conversation. It was becoming clearer with each mo-ment that Starlight was the kind of place Cory would be lucky to call her home. She tried not to think of how much Jordan was coming to mean to her. But after they drove home in companionable silence, they put Ben down for bed together, and to Cory it felt like they'd become a family. It felt like everything she'd secretly dreamed of, so when he drew her into his arms and then his bed, she let herself go with-out reservation.

"I've missed you, babe."

Cory whirled around at the sound of the familiar voice. The jar of pureed sweet potatoes she'd been taking from the shelf crashed to the floor and shattered. Chunks of orange goop splattered across the white squares of linoleum and onto her jeans.

"Still a klutz," Kade said with a smirk. "One of the things I love about you."

Her brain continued to have trouble with the fact that her ex-boyfriend was standing in a grocery aisle, so close she could reach out and touch him if she wanted. She didn't want to touch him or talk to him or even acknowledge his existence, although Kade was a hard man to ignore. His hair was close cropped, the way he'd always worn it, and he was dressed in a striped button-down, dark jeans and a leather jacket. No one could deny his raw masculinity, but seeing him only made Cory somewhat sick to her stomach.

She tried and mostly failed to calm her breathing as she looked past him to the grocery store clerk who'd appeared at the end of the aisle.

"I'm so sorry," she said to the older man even as she stepped in front of the cart that held her groceries and Ben. For some reason, she felt the need to put herself between her son and Kade. "It slipped from my fingers."

"We'll get it cleaned up in a jiffy," the clerk told her. His eyes widened as he realized who was standing with her. "My son and I loved watching you in the playoffs this year, Mr. Barrington."

Kade flashed his patented thousand-watt smile. "New England was a tough loss."

"You'll get them next year." The man pulled a cell phone from his pocket. "Would you be willing to take a selfie with me?"

"Sure thing," Kade said easily, then glanced at Cory. "Give me a minute."

She didn't answer, but there was no way she was giving her ex even one solitary second. As soon as Kade started toward the clerk, Cory unsnapped Ben's infant seat from the shopping cart and headed in the opposite direction, leaving her groceries deserted in the aisle.

She'd almost made it to her car when she heard the sound of footsteps jogging toward her.

"Babe, come on. Don't be like that. I came all this way."

She didn't break her stride. "For nothing, Kade. I don't want to talk to you like this."

"Then you should have texted me back." He caught up to her as she unlocked her car. "You didn't return my phone calls, either. I needed you after that last game. You're the only person I wanted with me."

"We're over." She opened the car door and bent forward to clip Ben's seat into the base. "We've been over for a while, Kade. Even before I left Atlanta. You know that."

"Is that our boy?"

Anger clawed at her throat, making it difficult to breathe. "He's not yours." She shut the car door and turned. "You know that, too."

"He could be." Kade gave a dismissive shrug, the diamond stud in his left ear glinting in the pale sunlight. It had rained overnight, so the air smelled like pine and forest even more than usual. She tried to let the scent calm her thudding heart.

"I'll give him my name," Kade told her like he was offering to bestow some kind of prize on her baby. "I'll give him everything you and I never had. All the things we wanted. The best schools, the biggest houses."

"That's not what I want for me or for my son." She shook her head. "It never has been."

"What do you want?" His expression tightened with obvious frustration.

"A happy life," she said simply. "What happened to the new girlfriend, Kade? I heard you were engaged."

"I broke it off because she wasn't you. We're still a part of each other, Cory." He reached around her and tapped his open palm to the peeling roof of the Buick. "You think you're going to get some fairy-tale happiness with Jordan Schaeffer?" Kade gave a dismissive sniff. "That guy was washed up before he even left the team. He had potential but no follow-through."

"How do you know about Jordan?" she demanded. "How did you even know where to find me?" She held up a hand before he could answer. "My mom told you." Kade was the only thing in Cory's life her mom approved of.

"At least she would talk to me." The irritation in his tone was clear. Kade had always been one for instant gratification, so Cory could imagine that not being able to immediately reach her had been a real problem.

Too bad his problems were no longer her concern.

"She shouldn't have done that," Cory said tightly, although it didn't surprise her. Even at Gran's funeral, Cory's mom had taken the opportunity to lecture her about how much she'd given up when she and Kade broke up.

"You're not a part of my life anymore," she told him, proud when her voice didn't waver. "You made it clear what it would take for me to stay in yours. I'm making choices for myself now. For my son." She pointed a finger at him. "Not yours, Kade. Mine."

"Give me a break." He shook his head. "I know you, Cory. I understand how you operate. You left me and went running home to your grandma, and when she was gone you decided your next best bet was latching on to Schaeffer. You never do anything for yourself."

The words hit like a series of blows. She knew in her rational mind that they weren't true, but in some ways, he was right. Cory should have never agreed to the pretend relationship with Jordan, but she had because it was easy to go along with what worked for somebody else. Because starting over in a new place totally on her own was terrifying, and relationships were her comfort zone. She knew how to be a daughter, a granddaughter, a girlfriend. What she'd never mastered was taking care of herself.

She'd thought she had a chance for a real change to how she did things in Starlight. At least that was what her plan had been. But her life here was based on a lie. Madison was the only person who knew the truth. Would her other friends stand by her when and if they realized her duplicity?

"Wow, your sweet words are really melting my heart." She glared at Kade. She might not be the best example of independence, but she didn't deserve to be shamed for it. "If I was such a needy, clingy drain on you, then what are you doing here?"

For a moment, there was a flicker of true emotion in his gaze. "Like I said, I miss you. You might be a train wreck, but you're my train wreck."

"I'm not yours," she said through gritted teeth. "And I'm not a train wreck. Not anymore."

"Sorry." He held up his hands. "I meant it as a compliment. I miss taking care of you. I miss having you waiting for me at the end of the night. I miss us."

"There is no us, Kade. I'm sorry you made the trip for—" She broke off, shook her head. "Scratch that. I'm not sorry. You coming here was your choice. I didn't ask for it, and I didn't invite you. Yes, I let you take care of me because it was easy. My mistake. I should have realized I don't need anyone to take care of me. In some ways I owe you, because leaving you taught me a lot about myself. I appreciate the history, but I'm not going to repeat. Not with you or any man."

"Come on, babe." Kade took a step closer but stopped when she held up a hand. "If you want something different, I'll give it to you. Whatever you want. Just say you'll try again."

"No."

He stared at her like he expected something more, but she just returned his gaze without emotion. Why had it taken her so long to realize that "no" was a complete sentence? She didn't owe him an explanation. She owed herself a chance.

He reached into the inside pocket of his leather jacket and pulled out an envelope, shoving it into her hand before she could protest. "I booked us a trip to Fiji. That's where you always wanted to go, remember? I've got time off. My agent wanted me to go right to a deodorant commercial shoot, but I said I've got to reconnect with my best girl first. I even hired a nanny for the kid and rented a separate condo for them. We'll have a real vacation, Cory. Just come with me and then you can decide about the future. Let's enjoy right now."

The scattered fragments of her resolve coalesced inside her until they obscured all of her doubts about her own strength. She wasn't the woman Kade wanted her to be. Maybe she never had been, only now she had the courage to step into the new version of herself. "I am enjoying my life right now," she told him. "I don't need a beach vacation to make me happy. Ben makes me happy. My life makes me happy." *And Jordan*, she wanted to add, but didn't. Because as happy as Jordan made her, Cory knew they had to go forward without anything fake between them if they were really going to have the chance she wanted.

It would be the first time in forever she hadn't taken the easy way out. But he was worth it. She was worth it.

"Good luck, Kade. I wish you the best, but you're not the best for me."

She climbed into her car and drove away. The envelope sat on the passenger seat, unopened. Maybe she should have forced him to take it back, but it didn't matter. She had no intention of using the ticket. Her life was here, and it was time she claimed it.

Chapter Sixteen

Jordan's heart plummeted to his toes as he pulled up to his house later that afternoon to witness Cory loading boxes into the back of her old sedan.

He'd come to love that automotive behemoth in the weeks she'd parked it in his driveway. It represented something about the woman and her quiet independence. At first, he'd offered daily to lease something new for her or to buy her a more reliable used car.

But she'd insisted she liked the Buick just fine, which was difficult to believe, because it drove like a tank. But Cory was proud and determined to do things on her own, and he respected her for it.

So why was she packing up now?

He refused to believe she didn't want to be with him. Not when their time together felt so right. He couldn't be the only one who sensed their bond deepening with every passing day. Yes, they talked about the time when they'd have to come clean about their relationship, but the longer it continued, the more certain he became that didn't have to be the only option.

They could be together for real.

He parked in front of the garage and got out of the truck, doing his best not to appear as alarmed as he felt.

"Cleaning out closets?" he asked with fake cheer.

"I'm leaving," she said as she closed the trunk.

"Leaving." He repeated the word numbly, feeling like he'd just taken a swift kick to the family jewels. His past had taught him not to reveal his emotions because that would give whoever was hurting him the upper hand. Whether with his father or on the line of scrimmage, Jordan never flinched.

He didn't shy away now, although his insides felt like they'd been sent through a meat grinder.

"What does that mean? You taking a girls' trip?"

"The pretend relationship ends now," she answered. "I'm going to stay with Tessa for a few days until I can make arrangements to rent my own place."

"You can't do that." He shook his head, grasping at anything that would keep her there. "We had an arrangement, Cory."

"Which we should have stopped when your mom left, Jordan. We both know it."

I don't know anything of the sort, his heart screamed. "Do we?" was his response.

"I told you from the start that I didn't seek you out because I had expectations. You deserved to know the truth about your son, and I wanted you to have a chance to have a relationship with him."

"How am I going to do that if you take him away?" he demanded, his voice cracking on the last word. He sucked in a breath and tried to muster some semblance of calm. "You can't take him from me, Cory."

"I wouldn't do that. Tessa's cabin is ten minutes away, and I'm not planning to leave Starlight. But I need to know I can make it on my own without having to rely on someone to take care of me."

He wanted to argue, to tell her that he was the one who needed her. That his house would be nothing more than a shell without her in it. That he loved her. But he didn't say any of those things. He'd spent his whole damn life hiding emotion because emotion made him weak, but somehow acting strong didn't make him feel any more in control at this moment.

Ben made a noise from inside the car.

"I have to go," Cory said gently. "I'm not walking away, Jordan."

"It sure looks like that from where I'm standing."

"I'll call you tomorrow," she said. "We can figure out how to start fresh. This isn't the end."

She went up on tiptoe to kiss him, but he turned his head so her mouth brushed his cheek. As angry as he was, he still wanted to kiss her. But he was half-afraid that if he let himself get close to her at this moment, he'd lose it.

He could feel her gaze on him but refused to look. After a few tense seconds, she squeezed his arm and moved away. He felt her absence like an icy wind. She could talk all she wanted about this not being the end, but watching her brake lights flash before she disappeared down his driveway, it sure felt like the end to Jordan.

Birds chirped in the trees overhead, and the afternoon sun warmed his shoulders. It seemed somehow wrong that the world could continue when it felt like his chest was splitting open and his heart would be irrevocably fractured.

After a few minutes, he went into the house. It was so damn quiet. Not the good kind of quiet, either. The kind that reminded him he was once again alone.

Unable to stand it on his own, he left for the bar. He arrived in the middle of happy hour, and the booths and tables were crowded with a mix of locals and out-of-towners. After greeting a few customers by name, Jordan headed for his office but made a detour for the bar when Tanya gestured him over.

"We've got a problem, boss."

He glanced over his shoulder at the groups of boisterous customers. "Tell me."

Before she could answer, a crash sounded from the kitchen, loud enough that people at several tables looked toward the swinging door that separated the two spaces.

"On second thought, don't tell me." He gave a small shake of his head. "I'll deal with it."

He entered the kitchen, which was filled with a tense silence only punctuated by the sizzling of the grill and the bubble from the fryer. In the past few weeks, since Cory's arrival, he'd gotten used to laughter and conversation among his staff as they worked.

Madison stood behind the stainless-steel counter, glaring down at a bowl of steaming pasta. "You'd better get out of my kitchen," she said without glancing up, "before I fillet you open like today's fresh catch."

"What happened to your new leaf and kinder, gentler personality?" Jordan asked, arching a brow.

"I'm kinder and gentler, just not to you." She met his gaze, pointed the tip of her knife in his direction. "You cost me my best employee."

Jordan blinked.

"Cory," she clarified, as if he couldn't tell who she was talking about. "She stopped in earlier and told me she was looking for a new job. The kitchen staff is supposed to be mine, Jordan. You're the boss of the front of the house. I run the back."

"I didn't fire Cory." He ran a hand through his

hair. "Hell, I didn't even know she was planning to quit."

The chef stepped around the prep counter and lowered her voice so that only he would hear her. "Doesn't that seem like something you should know about your own fiancée?" She gave him a hard stare.

"She didn't tell me. You can't blame me for something I didn't do."

"I'm not blaming you because she quit. I'm blaming you for making her want to."

"What does that even mean?"

"I know about your little arrangement," Madison said, leaning closer. "The truth. I'm the only one who knows the truth."

"Then why are you acting surprised this happened? It was bound to fall apart eventually."

She threw up her hands. "Only because you're an idiot. I don't care what Cory told me about the two of you being all for show when she first got to town. Things changed, didn't they?"

He pressed his lips together but gave a tight nod.

"You fell for her, and not just for pretend."

"What does it matter when she left?" He forced a breath when he realized he was starting to raise his voice. "She left me, and it looks like she left you."

"She quit the job in my kitchen." Madison inclined her head, giving him a funny look. "Yeah, it makes me mad because I liked working with her. She knew nothing about cooking, but she tried hard and never complained. Plus, she's a damn fine waitress. She and I will still be friends. The way she explained it to me, she ended the pretend part of your relationship. The part where you were playing house but not really committed. She wanted something real, and you wouldn't give it to her. She quit this job because she thinks it will be too hard to see you every day."

"That's ridiculous." He shook his head. "She knows I want her in my life for real. Hell, I put the toilet seat down after I flush."

Madison made a show of patting the pockets of her white chef's coat. "Too bad I'm fresh out of gold stars. You definitely qualify for one. Cory doesn't know you want to be with her for real."

"She should."

"Why?"

"Because I would never let anyone as close as she's gotten to me if I didn't want them for real."

"But did you tell her?"

"I didn't have to tell her," he insisted, although the argument sounded weak even to his ears. "I showed her."

"The testosterone in here is making it hard to breathe." Madison waved her fingers in front of her nose. "I'm gagging on your male stupidity."

"Not helpful," Jordan muttered.

"About as helpful as allowing a woman who's always considered herself a drain on the people she cares about to believe you were doing her a favor with your affection."

Jordan crossed his arms over his chest like that would protect him from the onslaught of the truth being hurled at him like spikes. "Let's not forget, she's the one who walked away."

Tanya came through the sliding door that led to the front of the bar and quickly approached. "Jordan, there's someone asking to talk to you."

"Can you handle it?" Jordan kept his gaze on Madison. "Comp their tab if you need to. We're in the middle of something important here." He had a feeling this conversation might help him fix the mess of his life.

"Kade Barrington just took a seat at the bar," Tanya said. "I don't think he's going to care that I buy him a drink."

Jordan's gut tightened. What the hell was Kade doing in Starlight? Did Cory know her ex-boyfriend had shown up in town? Something like panic niggled its way along his spine, but he pushed away the doubts. He couldn't allow himself to believe that her walking away earlier had anything to do with Kade.

"We're not finished," he told Madison.

"I've got cheese to fry," she answered and turned away. "But let me just mention I'll make a batch of your favorite cookies if you turn that rat-fink jerk out on his ear."

"No fighting," Tanya told him as they headed out of the kitchen.

"I break up fights," Jordan reminded her. "When have you ever known me to get in one?"

"I've never known you to be in love before Cory," Tanya answered. "Love changes everything."

Jordan muttered a curse. "Is it that obvious?"

"To everyone but the two of you, apparently."

Kade was sitting alone at the end of the bar as Jordan approached. It was the first time Jordan had ever seen the marquee quarterback without his crew of sycophants surrounding him. Somehow it made him look younger and less cocky than Jordan remembered.

No one in the bar paid him much mind, which was also strange, since Kade was a bona fide sports celebrity. Then he lifted his head and fixed his steel-blue gaze on Jordan, and the reason he was being left alone—as well as the reason for Tanya's warning about fighting—became clear. Kade Barrington had murder in his eyes.

"You're a long way from home," Jordan said casually, picking up a beer glass to dry as he moved closer.

"I'm here to collect what's mine," Kade said without preamble. "I'm not going home without her."

Jordan didn't pretend to misunderstand the other man. "Cory doesn't belong to you. She doesn't belong to anyone, and she gets to choose whether she stays or goes."

"You think she's going to choose you?"

"I think she's happy in Starlight."

"I can make her happier." Kade flicked his fingers across the bar. "I can give her way more than a small-time bar in a two-bit town. I can show her the world."

"Maybe she doesn't want to see it on your terms," Jordan suggested tightly. He was doing his best to keep a lid on his temper, but Kade's arrogance didn't make it an easy task.

"You had no right to touch her." Kade downed the remainder of the dark liquor and thumped the empty glass against the bar top. "Not then and not now."

"Again, it's her choice. Cory chooses who she allows close to her." He placed his hands on the edge of the bar and gripped it tight. "She chose me."

"Because I didn't want her at the time. Now I'm back, and she's coming with me. She's meant to be mine." Kade tapped a finger on the rim of his glass. "Another round."

"No." Jordan shook his head. He'd only had to kick a handful of customers out of the bar since he took ownership. Normally he could mitigate a situation before it came to that. He had no desire to defuse anything with Kade. Jordan wanted the cocky son of a gun gone before they both lost their tempers. "Go drink someplace else, Kade. Or better yet, go home to Atlanta. This isn't your place."

"I'll tell you where I'm going." Kade drew out an envelope from the inside of his coat. "I'm heading to the beach, and Cory's coming with me." He slapped a piece of paper that was clearly an itinerary with Cory's and Kade's names typed across the top. "You can't begin to hold a candle to what I can give her, Schaeffer. You're a washed-up former baller who's way past your prime, and your prime wasn't impressive to start."

Jordan couldn't seem to take his eyes from the paper with Cory's name printed alongside of Kade's. Was the timing of her moving out an actual coincidence, or could she be going to some fancy resort with her ex? Would she be swayed by the promise of some grand lifestyle? Jordan's dad had been kicking and screaming mad when Jordan retired and threw away the perks that came with being a professional athlete. He hadn't given a damn that Jordan didn't want to play the game anymore. It was like a knife to the gut to think Cory might feel the same.

"You know what your problem always was?" Kade grabbed the paper and shoved it back into his pocket. "You didn't have enough fight in you. Yeah, the coaches and management thought that was such an asset. They held you up as some sort of example because you're so cool and collected. No one ever figured out the reason. It's because you didn't really care. Not about the game or winning."

The other man laughed without humor. "You were meant for a smaller life," he chided. "But Cory deserves bigger and better. I'm going to give it to her."

"Get out, Kade." Jordan felt a muscle ticking in his jaw. He felt the buildup of pressure in his chest and knew he was close to the point of no return.

Kade climbed off the bar stool with a smirk, like he'd accomplished what he set out to do tonight. Jordan hated that he'd given the other man any satisfaction. "You know what else?" Kade's chest rose and fell with a deep breath. "I'm going to be the man who raises your son. God knows, the kid needs a fighting chance to turn out normal—not a quitter like his daddy."

Suddenly all Jordan could see was a red haze in front of him. The anger came swift and sure and practically knocked him sideways with its force. He didn't hesitate or think for one second before he stepped around the edge of the bar.

Kade immediately swung at him, but Jordan dodged the blow.

He threw a punch that landed with a satisfying crunch against Kade's perfect face. And all hell broke loose.

Cory arrived early for her first shift at Main Street Perk. She was scheduled to begin training at ten, and Tessa had agreed to watch Ben for the day when Jordan didn't return Cory's calls or texts the previous night.

His silence weighed on her and broke her heart even more than his casual indifference at her leaving. She believed him when he told her he wanted to be a big part of their son's life, and she hated to even consider that his feelings might change once she'd ended their fake relationship.

In truth, she'd hoped that her decision to move out would be a new beginning for them. Surely he knew what she felt about him. Surely he understood that the only way for them to truly be together was for him to freely choose her, not because of ease or some arbitrary necessity to put on a show for friends or family.

So why the radio silence?

"Hey, Mara," she said as the coffee shop manager and baker extraordinaire noticed her approaching the front counter.

"You're early." Mara glanced at her watch with a raised brow, then flashed a smile. "I like early."

"Does she ever," the dark-haired barista standing next to Mara said with a laugh. "Sometimes she thinks that because she's up at four in the morning to start baking, the rest of the world should follow suit."

"At least you work in a coffee shop," Cory said, feeling the heavy weight of her thoughts about Jordan start to lift. She'd reached out to Mara after she got settled at Tessa's and had been grateful when she received an immediate answer and job offer. "There's an endless supply of caffeine to get you through the day."

"Oh, she fizzles out right around two." The barista ignored Mara's eye roll and held out a hand to Cory. "I'm Ellen, and I'll be showing you the ropes today."

"Don't get your attitude from this one," Mara said, but she placed an arm around Ellen's shoulder and squeezed.

The small gesture made tears prick the backs of Cory's eyes. One of the things that had been the hardest about tendering her resignation with Madison was the thought of losing the connection between the kitchen staff. When she'd dated Kade, he hadn't wanted her to take a job that would compromise their time together, so she'd worked as a receptionist in the car dealership managed by the younger son of the team's owner. It was fine, but the connection to Kade ended up leaving her feeling like she had nothing that truly belonged to her.

Why had it taken her so long to realize she deserved that?

"You won't have to worry about my attitude," Cory promised, trying for a laugh, which came out more like a sob.

"Okay." Mara grimaced. "Why don't we start with a tour of the kitchen?"

Ellen, who clearly hadn't noticed Cory's upset,

gave her boss a funny look. "Don't you think we should start with the cappuccino machine while we aren't too busy?"

"That's fine," Cory said, and drat if her voice didn't crack again.

"It will just take a few minutes," Mara told the barista, then crooked a finger at Cory. "First rule of Perk. Do what the boss tells you."

That earned a genuine laugh from Cory. "You might have a few things in common with Madison."

"Don't say that again," Mara said at the same time Ellen whispered, "I like this one."

Cory followed Mara into the kitchen. Unlike the back of the house at Trophy Room, this space smelled like sugar and butter. Cory breathed deeply. "This is how I imagine the scent of a perfect childhood. Your daughter must love it here."

"She does." Mara grabbed a snickerdoodle from the cooling rack and shoved it toward Cory. "What's the problem?"

"There's no problem."

"If my baristas are choking back tears in front of customers, that's a problem."

Cory popped a bite of cookie into her mouth. "I have allergies."

"Do they have to do with Jordan beating the crap out of Kade Barrington last night at the bar?"

Cory choked on the cookie. "What are you talking about? Was Jordan hurt?"

Mara gave her a hard pat on the back, then turned to fill up a glass of water. She handed Cory the glass. "The way I heard it, Jordan took care of business. I assumed you knew." She leaned in. "The way I heard it, their beef had something to do with an old grudge from the days they played together back in Atlanta. But I think there's more to the story. You're that more."

Cory took a long drink of water and then wiped a hand across her mouth. All the while, her mind whirled with the idea of Jordan and Kade getting in a fistfight and the fact that it could have anything to do with her.

"I don't…" She wanted to deny it but couldn't bring herself to tell another lie to someone in this town she cared about or might one day consider a friend. "I don't know how to keep pretending like I know what I'm doing."

"You don't have to have all the answers," Mara said gently.

Cory gave a shaky nod and shoved the last piece of cookie into her mouth. "No chance of that," she admitted. "I have no idea what happened at the bar. Kade showed up in town yesterday, but I sent him away. I didn't think he'd seek out Jordan. Who, by the way, doesn't seem to be speaking to me at the moment. My life's a mess."

"Messes can be cleaned up," Mara said. "Trust me."

"Would it be okay if I just got to work? Right now I need a distraction, and I promise no tears."

Mara studied her for a long moment. "Sure," she said finally. "And if you're going to cry, come back here. Free cookies for your first day on the job."

"I might take you up on that. Now I'd like to learn how to make a fancy coffee."

Chapter Seventeen

Jordan parked his car in front of the small cabin tucked away in the trees and wished that a million things were different in his life at the moment. Most of all, he wished that Cory wasn't coming down the front steps holding his baby and an overnight bag to give to him.

The soft pink sweatshirt she wore highlighted her creamy skin, and her hair was pinned back from her face in jeweled barrettes. She offered a tentative smile as she got closer, but the smile faded when she took in the bruise that darkened his left eye. "What happened to you?"

He shrugged and reached out a hand to smooth

it over Ben's head. The boy gave him a wide, tooth-less grin, then curled shyly into his mother's chest, which made Jordan's chest ache. "Things got a little out of hand at the bar. No big deal."

"Did that out of hand involve Kade?" she asked quietly.

Jordan couldn't read her expression. "If you're asking, then I think you know it did. Word travels fast in a small town. And Kade did more than his share of talking last night."

Her mouth thinned, and she glanced away. "I hope you didn't believe him."

"You're still here. If he'd been telling me the truth, you'd be on your way to Fiji by now, along with Ben."

"Things are over between Kade and me," she said. "They have been for a long time."

"Does he know that?"

"He does now."

Jordan nodded slowly and thought about what to say next. The truth was he didn't want to say any-thing. He wanted to pull Cory into his arms and hold her close. He wanted to breathe in the scent of her hair and feel the warmth of her body pressed against his. He hated the distance between them and the way she wouldn't hold his gaze. "I wondered at the tim-ing of you ending things between us and then Kade showing up at Trophy Room. Had you seen him be-fore you left?"

She gave a tight nod. "But Kade isn't the reason I

moved out of your house, Jordan. Although, talking to him did make me realize some things about how I want my life to be."

"And I take it that doesn't involve any football players, ex or current?"

Her brows drew together like she didn't understand the question. "I want to make a good life for my son."

"Our son." Ben decided at that moment that Jordan passed the familiarity test and reached for him. As soon as he took the boy into his arms, emotion clogged his throat. "I missed you, buddy. We're going to hit it hard tonight. Maybe even peas and pears for dinner."

He felt a ridiculously inflated sense of pride when Cory laughed at his corny joke.

She passed him the diaper bag and duffel she'd packed. "If you need anything, call me. This is the first time since he came home after his surgery that I've been away from him for the night." She swiped at her cheeks. "It's going to be strange."

"It doesn't have to be like this," Jordan told her.

She shook her head. "I'm done pretending."

He almost staggered back a step at those three words. Was that all he meant to her, really? A pretend relationship that she no longer wanted or needed?

"Okay, then. That makes it clear." He turned and secured the baby into the car seat, stowing the bags
~he floor of the truck. "I'll call you tomorrow

about dropping him off. Thanks for letting me keep him for the night, Cory. I guess…" He rubbed a hand over the back of his neck. "We'll have to come up with a more formal custody agreement going forward."

"Yeah," she agreed and swallowed hard. "I'm hoping to get more hours at the coffee shop after I finish training." She looked at the ground. "I ordered some supplies to start making more jewelry. I'm going to try to get enough inventory to participate in the Dennison Mill event, and whatever's left over I'll list online. That should bring in some extra cash, and it's something I can do at night while Ben's sleeping."

"I don't want you to worry about money," Jordan told her. "If you need anything, I can help."

"I want to make it on my own."

"But child support is a thing, right?" He shook his head. "It feels like we're going at this all backward. I want to support you and Ben."

"You don't owe me anything," she reminded him.

"I do," he countered. He wanted to say more. He wanted to disagree and tell her he owed her for bringing him back to life. For making him see that there was so much more happiness available to him if he just was brave enough to reach out and take it.

"Cory, I—"

"I should let you get going." She crossed her arms over her chest when a breeze kicked up.

"How are things going at Main Street Perk?"

"Good." She drew in a breath. "Everyone is really nice."

"Madison is distraught without you. She blames me."

That earned a half smile. "She knows it was my decision. She just likes giving you grief."

"Good to know. I guess I'll talk to you later, then."

"I'm a call away if you need me." She bit down on her lower lip. "If Ben needs anything."

An important distinction, Jordan supposed, because it felt like he needed her more than he needed his next breath. But he didn't know how to say that and not risk having his heart crushed into a million pieces, so he just nodded, got in his truck and drove away.

The panic set in seconds later. Panic at the realization that he was responsible for Ben for the next twenty-four hours. Without hesitating, he picked up his phone and hit the number to call his mom.

She answered on the first ring.

"I messed up bad," he told her and then proceeded to explain the entire situation from the beginning. Cory's arrival in Starlight. His idea for the pretend relationship at the funeral and how that led to an extended ruse when Kathy announced her plans for a visit. His feelings for Cory were real, even if their relationship had started out fake.

His mother listened to his entire story, then immediately lectured him on making a call while behind the wheel and the dangers of distracted driving. For some reason, that small bit of maternal scolding relaxed him more than he would have imagined.

"Okay, I'm home," he told her as he pulled into the garage. "Will you tell me how to fix things now?" He cradled the phone between his cheek and shoulder as he got Ben out of the car and headed into the house.

"Do you love her?" his mother asked like it was the easiest question in the world to answer.

And suddenly it was. "Yes," he told her. "I love her so much it hurts."

"Have you told her?"

"Oh, hell no."

"No cursing, young man. And do you see the problem with that?"

"Not one bit. What if she doesn't feel the same? She told me she was done pretending, Mom. Those exact words. How can I tell her and risk freaking her out? And what if I freak her out so much that she doesn't want to let me be part of Ben's life?"

"Wow," his mom murmured with a soft laugh. "Those are a lot of potential issues."

"Exactly."

"I never took my son for a coward."

He paused, held the phone in front of him, unsure he'd heard her right. "How does being cautious suddenly translate into being a coward?"

"I don't know your Cory well," his mother answered, "but she didn't strike me as the kind of

woman who would keep you from having a relationship with your son. Do you really believe that?"

"No," he admitted. "She would never use Ben
that way."

"Good. And did it ever occur to you she might be
having the same worries as you?"

"She's the one who walked away."

"Did you give her another option?"

"Yes. I told her…" Jordan broke off and thought
about what he had and hadn't told Cory over the past
few weeks. "She knows how I feel."

"Because she's a mind reader or because she has
such a great track record with men in her life doing
the right thing?"

"I'm not like Kade or her dad or any other guy
who's treated her like she doesn't matter," Jordan
insisted.

"Then show her," his mom urged. "Tell her. I saw
the two of you together, Jordan. There's something
special there. Now you both just have to be willing
to go after it. You've always pursued what you want,
son. Don't let this be any different."

"Thanks, Mom." He placed Ben on a blanket and
sank down next to him on the carpet. "I appreciate
the advice. I should go now."

"Maybe you could plan a weekend to drive over
to Spokane?" His mom's confident tone had suddenly gone tentative.

"That would be great." Jordan blew out a rush of

air. Never would he have imagined himself in the position to want his mother to be a part of his life, but it felt strangely right now. It felt real and right.

"Don't cry."

Cory met Madison's steely gaze and nodded. "I'm holding it together."

"I swear, I won't let you in my kitchen again if you cry."

Cory and Tessa had arrived at Madison's near downtown Starlight twenty minutes earlier. The house was a charming Craftsman style, with glowing fir floors, lots of built-ins and a brick fireplace in the living room. The kitchen was small but had beautiful butcher-block counters and stainless appliances. Madison's home felt welcoming and cozy, and it was like getting a peek inside the secret soul of the hard-nosed chef.

They hadn't had a club meeting scheduled, but Tessa took one look at Cory's face after Jordan and Ben drove away and called an emergency session.

They were making enchiladas because Madison deemed them the ultimate comfort food.

"She's not going to cry," Ella said and wrapped an arm around Cory's shoulder before glancing at her. "Oh, she's totally going to cry."

"Think about something happy," Tessa advised.

"All of my happy thoughts involve Ben," Cory

said, and then her voice broke. Her throat and eyes burned with the effort of holding back the ears.

"Think about cute puppies and kittens," Tessa advised with a cheery smile. "That always helps me feel better."

"But don't think about those humane-society commercials with the abused animals," Madison added as she whisked the cheese sauce heating over a gas burner on the stove. "Those are a total downer."

Cory let out a laugh that quickly turned into a strangled sob. "You give the worst pep talks in the history of the world."

The other woman shrugged. "Pep talks aren't in my wheelhouse. But these enchiladas are going to blow your mind."

"Shouldn't we be helping?" Tessa asked and then plucked a chip from the bowl on the counter and dunked it into Madison's homemade salsa. "I thought the point of this was for us to learn."

"We're learning by osmosis," Ella said and then took a long pull on her beer. "Besides, I'm not sure there are any men out there even worth learning to cook for. That just supports the patriarchy."

"Jordan appreciated when I tried to make dinner," Cory said with another sniff. "Even though I wasn't good at it. He did plenty of the cooking and always brought me coffee in the morning. He was perfect."

"Jordan Schaeffer is not perfect," Madison said,

then bobbed her eyebrows. "Okay, physically he's perfect, but he has faults."

Ella squeezed Cory's shoulders. "Top of the list is that he let you walk away."

"Exactly," Madison agreed.

To Cory's surprise, Tessa shook her head. "Not so fast. I'm not sure I agree that's a fault. Maybe it's because my mom was a big Sting fan, but I think his sage words of 'if you love someone, set them free' ring true in this case." She threw up her hands when Cory, Ella and Madison just stared at her. "Come on—you know what I'm talking about. 'Free, free, set them free,'" she sang in a ferociously off-key soprano.

"Sting is great for an old guy," Madison agreed.

"Also still hot," Tessa added, tipping her wineglass to drain it.

"Kind of gross, but okay." Madison poured the sauce over the rolled enchiladas and popped the baking dish into the oven. "But Jordan should have fought for our girl."

Tessa wrinkled her nose, clearly disagreeing. "Maybe he thought she wanted him to let her go, and that he was doing the right thing by her."

"Whose side are you on?" Cory asked, feeling miserable.

Tessa frowned. "Yours. Whose side are you on, Cory?" She stepped around the counter and squared her shoulders. "Because I've heard you crying in your bedroom the past few nights when you should be asleep. I've listened to you talk about happiness and making a good life for Ben, but isn't part of that having the cojones to go after what you want?"

"I have cojones," Cory muttered.

"You love Jordan."

Cory drew in a breath, wanting to deny it. As reserved as Tessa could be, she'd picked an interesting time to grow a backbone. "I do."

"But you won't tell him."

"I don't want to give him a chance to hurt me."

"Give the man more credit," Tessa insisted.

"She has a point," Ella said. "Plus, if a man made me coffee every morning, I'd never let him go."

"That's the problem," Cory told them. "I don't want to let him go. Ever. I see a future with Jordan. The kind of future I desperately want. I didn't even know I could want something so badly, that I could love a person other than Ben so much. It scares me, because love makes me weak."

"That's a fact," Ella said.

"Amen, sister," Madison added.

"No." Tessa shook her head. "The right kind of love makes you strong. It makes you brave enough to take on anything, because you know you'll have a soft place to land at the end of the day. Just because all of you have been hurt before, that doesn't make love bad. It means you have to make better choices the next time around."

"I choose Ben and Jerry," Ella said.

"And Henry Cavill in that show where he's got the long hair and leather pants," Madison said with a sigh. "I don't need any other man."

Tessa gave Madison a pointed look. The chef turned to Cory. "I agree Jordan is a good guy. And he obviously cares about you and Ben. I mean, you could do worse."

"High praise," Ella said with a laugh.

"I told him I don't want a pretend relationship," Cory argued. "I can't go crawling back to him now."

"Your feelings aren't pretend, honey." Ella's smile was gentle. "Neither are his. That changes everything."

"Love changes everything." Tessa nodded.

Cory's nerves buzzed with the idea that she could actually go after a second chance—or possibly a third chance—with Jordan. She realized she wanted everything Tessa was talking about, and she wanted it with Jordan.

Now the question was how to make it happen.

Chapter Eighteen

Jordan had planned to talk to Cory when she came to pick up Ben the previous night. He'd had flowers and sweets at the house all ready to go as olive branches or tokens of his affection or...well, he hoped the gifts could communicate what Jordan hadn't figured out a way to say.

He didn't even know her favorite flower, but he'd figured he'd go with the classic staples of roses and a box of chocolates for wooing a woman. In truth, he had no clue how to woo a woman. He'd never cared enough to try.

Cory was worth wooing. She meant everything to him, and he desperately wanted a chance to prove it.

But now it was Saturday morning and the flowers sat wilting on the counter, much like his self-confidence. When she'd come by last night, she'd been tense and stressed about her booth at the Dennison Mill market. He'd also seen a sense of determination in her. It was clear that Cory was different from the uncertain woman she'd been when she arrived in Starlight. She was coming into herself, and he didn't want to take a chance on derailing or distracting her from the life she was building in town.

He wanted her to be happy more than he wanted her for himself.

If it wasn't so pathetic, he'd laugh at his skill at rationalizing his cowardice. He was afraid to give her a chance to reject him outright. His mother would have counseled him that it was worth the risk. Madison and Tanya would probably have told him to pull up his big-boy boxers and stop acting like a wuss.

Cory had texted him late last night, asking if he would pick up Ben from Tessa's house that morning because she had to set up early. He'd agreed but now regretted not saying more.

So many regrets. Jordan hated regrets.

He grabbed his phone from the counter and sent a message wishing her luck and then asked if she would have dinner with him after the market. Baby steps were better than nothing, right? He waited with his breath held as the three little dots flashed on the screen while she typed her reply.

Yes on dinner. Thank you for the luck. I'll need it.

That was a start, he thought, trying not to be disappointed she hadn't messaged him more. It felt ridiculous that he wasn't with her to offer support in person. His mom's words about going after what he wanted echoed through his mind. Jordan wanted a chance at a real future with Cory and Ben.

His phone dinged and he checked it, the message sending a jolt of emotion through his body.

She'd sent him a red heart emoji.

And suddenly that one colorful shape changed everything inside Jordan. He'd been a fool and a coward, just like his mom had gently admonished. He was so busy trying to protect himself from being hurt, he hadn't realized he was only hurting himself.

He hurriedly typed in his reply.

You're going to do amazing today. You are amazing, Cory. I can't wait to see you shine.

He went to hit Send, then added his own heart emoji. God, he felt like a lovesick schoolboy.

As he drove to Tessa's, he came up with and rejected nearly a dozen plans for how to show Cory what she meant to him. What he needed was a night to binge-watch all the rom-com movies ever made for inspiration.

He could borrow an old-school boom box from

someone in town. There might even be one in the bar's storage room.

No, that was stupid.

What about serenading her? Only problem was Jordan couldn't carry a tune to save his life.

Maybe he'd borrow the classic "you complete me" line. She did, as far as he was concerned, but he didn't want to recycle someone else's moment for his.

He'd worked himself into quite the emotional frenzy by the time Tessa answered the door.

"What's wrong with you?" she asked, taking a step back like he was a feral animal. She held Ben a little closer. "Your eyes aren't right."

"What's wrong is that I miss Cory like I've lost a piece of my heart. I'm going to fix things with her," he vowed, his voice sounding panicked even to his own ears. "I have to fix it."

Ben turned at the sound of his daddy's voice and gave an excited squeal. At least the baby wasn't wary of him this morning. Jordan didn't hesitate in reaching for his son, and his heart slowed a bit in its frantic thudding when Ben cuddled against his shoulder. "I need help," he said to Cory's friend.

The pretty redhead nodded. "You don't ask for help easily."

"I never ask anyone for help," he clarified. "But my usual way isn't working. I'm kind of desperate here."

One corner of her mouth curved. "You love her."

"More than I ever could have imagined. She's everything to me."

Tessa's grin widened. "Did you consider telling her that? It's pretty convincing."

He shrugged and looked out to the wild expanse of forest surrounding the cabin. "What if it's not enough?" he asked, then added, "What if I'm not enough? If I can do something huge and flashy to convince her…"

"Jordan, stop." Tessa placed a gentle hand on his arm. "Do you understand how much time she's put into getting ready for today's market?"

He glanced back at her. "A lot."

"A whole lot. And it made her happy. Being with you and Ben as a family made her happy. If Cory wanted flashy, she'd be on a beach in Fiji with that tool ex of hers. I can't guarantee what she'll say if you tell her how you feel, but I think the risk of truly showing her your heart will be worth it in the end. I can tell you have a good heart, Jordan."

He blew out an unsteady breath. "Emotional risk isn't exactly something I excel at, you know?"

"I can appreciate that." She winked. "It also wouldn't hurt to ask Madison to whip up a batch of fried cheese. Cory's kind of a goner when it comes to cheese. It's the little things."

"The little things," he repeated as an idea dawned on him. "Thank you, Tessa." He leaned in for a quick hug. "You eat and drink on the house at Trophy Room for all of eternity if this works out."

Her mouth dropped open, and then she gave a ladylike fist pump. "I like the sound of that."

As Jordan walked to his truck, his mind whirled with everything he needed to do before he headed toward the market. Today he was going to show Cory how much she meant to him in a way that he hoped would mean as much to her.

Cory surveyed the empty table in front of her with a happy heart. The Dennison Mill Maker's Market had been a huge success. Crowds of shoppers had browsed the booths situated around the large courtyard, and Cory had catered to a constant stream of customers. She'd sold every piece of jewelry she brought with her and had orders from almost two dozen women for additional items.

The weather had been perfect, sunny and warm with the scent of spring in the air. She wasn't sure if the beautiful day had brought so many people to the shopping and dining area or if Brynn was truly some kind of small-town marketing genius.

Either way, the pride Cory felt in what she'd accomplished nearly brought tears to her eyes. She finally was certain she'd found the life she wanted in Starlight.

She'd been too afraid to trust that something good could happen to her, too scared to go after her dreams.

No more excuses and no more letting other people's expectations guide her life.

She was making her own choice on her terms.

As Gran would tell her, Cory had the power to figure it out. And next on the list was determining how to make that happen with Jordan at her side.

She'd found herself in Starlight—true friends and a real community. She'd discovered a home.

But it was incomplete without Jordan.

She was incomplete without him.

For the first time, loving another person didn't make her feel weak or like she was giving up too much of herself. Her love for Jordan—and the way he loved her in return—made her strong. She believed with her whole heart that being with him would give her a foundation from which to build her life into something even better.

Okay, he hadn't exactly told her he loved her.

But he'd shown her in so many ways that meant the world to Cory. He listened to her and supported her, even when he didn't necessarily agree with her choices. He let her make her own choices. She had to trust that his actions counted for something. She knew how hard it was for him to talk about his feelings, just like it was for her.

But they could get through that. She wasn't going to give up on him, and not just because they shared a son. Jordan was her other half.

She shook her head as she started to pack up her

empty display fixtures. No, that wasn't right. She was whole on her own. But he complemented the person she wanted to be. He'd helped her find the strength to be that person. Cory bent over to pick up a piece of ribbon that had dropped on the ground next to her chair.

"Looks like you finished strong."

Lost in thought, she startled at the sound of his deep voice, banging her head on the table. "Ouch." She mustered a smile as she straightened. There were still vendors talking to customers on either side of her booth, but when her eyes met Jordan's, it somehow felt like they were the only two people on the planet. Well, three people, since he was holding their sweet baby.

"Are you okay?" he asked, his gaze searching hers, gentle and almost cautious.

"Just tired," she said, rubbing the back of her head. "My blood sugar could use a boost, as well. I haven't eaten since you brought me the salad for lunch. Thank you, by the way. And for watching Ben." She pushed back from the table. "If you have other things to do…" She broke off. This was not how she wanted things to go between them. Passing the baby back and forth. She wanted to be a family. "I'm glad you were here, Jordan. It meant a lot to me."

He seemed to suck in an unsteady breath before flashing the grin that always made her knees go weak. "There's no place I'd rather be, and I'm happy to spend the day with our son." He glanced over his shoulder, then back at her, and she had trouble reading his expression.

"What's going on?" she asked.

"Could you come with me for a minute?" His smile faltered slightly. "I wanted to talk to you and to show you something."

"I have to get my booth cleaned up, but then—"

"Sure, she can go with you," Tessa said as she and Ella materialized at his side.

Cory frowned. "Were you two hiding behind him to eavesdrop?"

"Of course not." Ella reached for the baby. "But you do look like you need some food. We'll take care of packing the rest of your stuff, and I'm happy to hang out with my favorite little man." She nuzzled Ben's neck, and the baby giggled with delight.

Cory couldn't understand what was happening. She felt the weight of Jordan's gaze, and her body went on full alert. Awareness pulsed through her veins like a double shot of espresso, but she kept her features neutral.

"Okay," she said slowly as she shifted her gaze to her two friends, both of whom looked far too innocent. "But if you're letting him lead me off for some nefarious purposes, I'll tell you right now that paybacks are hell."

"Duly noted," Ella said.

Tessa yanked her around the side of the table. "Get going, you two."

"That didn't go quite as smoothly as I planned," Jordan told her as she fell into step next to him. He led her around the corner of the old mill building.

She cocked a brow and glanced up at him. "You have a plan?"

"It's evolving," he admitted. "But yes."

They got to the back of the building, and her mouth fell open.

The flagstone courtyard that flanked the building had been strewn with fairy lights, and a round wrought-iron table sat in the middle of the patio.

Madison, who was lighting a candle situated in the center of the table, turned as they approached and muttered several colorful curses before grinning at Cory. "Sorry, I'm supposed to be gone by now. Have fun."

Before Cory could respond, her friend darted past and then called over her shoulder, "Always remember, chicks before...well, you know."

Cory turned to Jordan. "Why do I feel like I don't actually know anything right now?"

"Evolving," he said with a grimace. "But stick with me, okay?"

He looked so uncharacteristically discombobulated, Cory couldn't help but smile. "Yeah," she whispered. "I'll stick with you."

Jordan must have heard the unspoken promise in

those words, because he visibly relaxed as he linked his fingers with hers and moved toward the table.

"I have some things I need to say to you," he told her. "And a gift that goes with each one." He squeezed her hand. "It's not flowers or chocolate or anything all that mind-blowing, but…"

"Let me be the judge of what blows my mind," she told him.

He led her to one of the chairs and grabbed a small striped gift bag from the table as she sat. "First I want to tell you I'm sorry." He handed her the bag. "I'm sorry I made you feel like I was giving up on us. I let my fears and doubts get in the way. I won't do that again, Cory. No matter what you decide, I'm not leaving or running away. You can trust me with your heart. I promise that."

She struggled to catch her breath as the magnitude of his words rushed over her. "Jordan, I—"

"Open the first gift," he said.

She dug through the tissue paper and pulled out a garage door opener. "Um, thanks?"

His cheeks bloomed with color. "There's a key chain in there, too. It has two keys on it. One for my house and one for the bar. Everything that's mine is now yours. I want to come home to you. I want to be the man you come home to." He knelt down in front of her. "You are my home in every way that counts. I love you, Cory."

Was it possible for a heart to actually burst from

happiness? Because that was the only explanation for what was happening inside Cory. Her heart pounded so loudly she couldn't even hear herself think.

But she didn't need to think. All she needed was to feel the joy of this moment. She leaned forward and wrapped her arms around Jordan's neck.

"I love you," she said, then kissed him with an intensity that made her forget her own name. After several minutes, she pulled back and stared into his captivating green eyes. The same eyes as their son. "I'm yours, Jordan, and you are mine. Whatever life brings us, we're in it together."

"So the garage door opener was better than flowers?" he asked with a self-satisfied smile. "I can't wait to tell Madison."

"It worked for me," she told him, then kissed him again.

"I have one more gift," he said. "Also not flowers." He reached into his pocket and pulled out a velvet box.

Cory's breath hitched again.

His smile turned tender. "My mom left this with me," he explained. "She noticed that you didn't have a proper engagement ring."

"We weren't properly engaged," Cory couldn't help but point out.

"I want to change that." Jordan opened the box to reveal a pear-shaped diamond set in a delicate band of gold filigree. "This belonged to my great-grandmother. She and my great-grandpa were married fifty-eight years, and family legend goes, he loved her more every day. That's what I want, Cory. That's my vow. I'll be your partner. I'll be the best dad I can to Ben and to any other children who bless our lives. I'll be whatever you need me to be, because you are my everything. Will you marry me?"

Tears streamed down her face as he slipped the ring onto her finger. "Yes. I'll be your wife and your partner and your friend for always, Jordan. I'm all in."

They kissed again, and Cory knew that she was well and truly home.

* * * * *

For more romance featuring charming kids,
try these other great stories:

Their Second-Time Valentine
by Helen Lacey

Wyoming Cinderella
by Melissa Senate

A Firehouse Christmas Baby
by Teri Wilson

Available now from Harlequin Special Edition!

WE HOPE YOU ENJOYED
THIS BOOK FROM

Believe in love. Overcome obstacles. Find happiness.

Relate to finding comfort and strength in the
support of loved ones and enjoy the journey
no matter what life throws your way.

6 NEW BOOKS AVAILABLE EVERY MONTH!

#2827 RUNAWAY GROOM

The Fortunes of Texas: The Hotel Fortune • by Lynne Marshall

When Mark Mendoza discovers his fiancée cheating on him on their wedding day, he hightails it out of town. Megan Fortune is there to pick up the pieces—and to act as his faux girlfriend when his ex shows up. Mark swears he will never get involved again. Megan doesn't want to be a "rebound" fling. But they find each other irresistible. What's a fake couple to do?

#2828 A NEW FOUNDATION

Bainbridge House • by Rochelle Alers

While restoring a hotel with his adoptive siblings, engineer Taylor Williamson hires architectural historian Sonja Rios-Martin. Neither of them ever thought they'd mix business with pleasure, but when their relationship runs into both of their pasts, they'll have to figure out if this passion is worth fighting for.

#2829 WYOMING MATCHMAKER

Dawson Family Ranch • by Melissa Senate

Divorced real estate agent Danica Dunbar still isn't ready for marriage and motherhood. When she has to care for her infant niece, Ford Dawson, the sexy detective who wants to settle down, is a little too helpful. Will this matchmaker pawn him off on someone else? Or is she about to make a match of her own?

#2830 THE RANCHER'S PROMISE

Match Made in Haven • by Brenda Harlen

Mitchell Gilmore was best man at Lindsay Delgado's wedding, "uncle" to her children and, when Lindsay is tragically widowed, a consoling shoulder. Until one electric kiss changes everything. Now Mitchell is determined to move from lifelong friendship to forever family. It's a risky proposition, but maybe Lindsay will finally make good on her promise.

#2831 THE TROUBLE WITH PICKET FENCES

Lovestruck, Vermont • by Teri Wilson

A pregnant former beauty queen and a veteran fire captain at the end of his rope realize it's never too late to build a family and that life, love and lemonade are sweeter when you let down your guard and open your heart to fate's most unexpected twists and turns.

#2832 THEIR SECOND-CHANCE BABY

The Parent Portal • by Tara Taylor Quinn

Annie Morgan needs her ex-husband's help—specifically, she needs him to sign over his rights to the embryos they had frozen prior to their divorce. But when she ends up pregnant—with twins—it becomes very clear their old feelings never left. Will their previous problems wreck their relationship once again?

*Mitchell Gilmore and Lindsay Delgado had been best
friends for as long as they could remember. He was
best man at her wedding, "uncle" to her children
and, when Lindsay is tragically widowed, a consoling
shoulder. Until one electric kiss changes everything.
Now Mitchell is determined to move from lifelong
friendship to forever family—if Lindsay can see that
he's ready to be a family man...*

Read on for a sneak peek at
The Rancher's Promise
*by Brenda Harlen,
the new book in her Match Made in Haven series!*

"Do you want coffee?" Lindsay asked.

"No, thanks."

"So…how was your date?"

Considering that it was over before nine o'clock,
she was surprised when Mitchell said, "Actually, it was
great. It turns out that Karli's not just beautiful but smart
and witty and fun. We had a great dinner and interesting
conversation."

She didn't particularly want to hear all the details, but
she'd been the one to insist they remain firmly within the
friend zone and, as a friend, it was her duty to listen.

"That is great," she said. Lied. "I'm happy for you." Another lie. "But I have to wonder, if she's so great… why are you here?"

"Because she's not you," he said simply. "And I don't want anyone but you."

She might have resisted the words, but the intensity and sincerity of his gaze sent them arrowing straight to her heart. Still, she had to be smart. To think about what was at stake.

"I know you're afraid to risk our friendship, and I understand why. But there's so much more we could have together. So much more we could be to one another. Don't we deserve a chance to find out?"

Before Lindsay could respond to either his confession or his question, he was kissing her.

Don't miss
The Rancher's Promise *by Brenda Harlen,*
available April 2021 wherever
Harlequin Special Edition books and ebooks are sold.

Harlequin.com

HSEEXP0321

Love Harlequin romance?

DISCOVER.

Be the first to find out about promotions, news and exclusive content!

f Facebook.com/HarlequinBooks

🐦 Twitter.com/HarlequinBooks

📷 Instagram.com/HarlequinBooks

📌 Pinterest.com/HarlequinBooks

ReaderService.com

EXPLORE.

Sign up for the Harlequin e-newsletter and download a free book from any series at **TryHarlequin.com**

CONNECT.

Join our Harlequin community to share your thoughts and connect with other romance readers!
Facebook.com/groups/HarlequinConnection

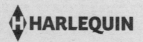

HSOCIAL2020